The Summer Job

A Siobhan Murphy Adventure

Margaret Cioffi

Black Rose writing™

First printing

ISBN: 978-1-61296-555-0
PUBLISHED BY BLACK ROSE WRITING
www.blackrosewriting.com

Printed in the United States of America
Suggested retail price $16.95

The Summer Job is printed in Gentium Book Basic

To Mary Pat and Joanne. Love.

The Summer Job

Chapter 1

Hi, my name is Siobhan Murphy I'm sixteen years old, I'm a student and live with my parents Mary and Pat Murphy. I'm it, in terms of children, and I'll probably live with my folks until I either get married or get a job offer in Machu Pichu. Don't get me wrong, I actually like living with my folks, they're terrific, they don't bug me and I really enjoy spending time with them. My mother is a library assistant and my Dad is a postal worker, ordinary people who want the very best for yours truly. I know they would give me anything I asked for, but I can't imagine taking anything more from them than what they already give me. I know that sounds pretty sappy, but it's true. Both my parents would take on another job if I asked them for help with my college tuition, or anything else that costs a lot. I've got another year to go before the whole college thing happens but I want to start now saving as much money as I can. I want to pay for as much if not all of my college education myself. Earning the morning shouldn't be all that hard with summer and part time jobs, it the saving that's seriously tough because I've got a serious case of spenditis. I have money in my pocket, spot something I want and before I know it, boom, my money is gone and what I bought is on its way home with me.

School is out for the summer, and I absolutely have to find the best summer job, paying the most money that I could possibly make. If I don't land a totally kick butt job I'll be stacking up student loans like cups at Starbucks. I never quite figured out how early in the school year you should begin your quest for a summer job. Me, I've always waited until the end of the school year to begin my job search, that way I would be totally focused on getting a good job. So far I've never managed to land anything that would be considered 'kick butt'. This year would be different. This year I am on a mission.

Every year since I was old enough to work at a summer job, I've only ever managed to get crappy jobs, making crappy money, and at the end of the summer, regardless of how hard I try to save, I have almost nothing left for the school year. If you asked me what my dream summer job was I would have to say camp counselor, I'm not sure why, being a camp counselor is totally not me, but there you have it. You know the type of jobs I'm talking about, great outdoors, rustic, gung-ho type jobs. The lucky kids that get camp counselor jobs get to leave the city for the entire summer, wear khaki shorts and t-shirts emblazoned with the camp name; usually some sort of name like Camp Kikishitshit or something. They spend their summers working at a rustic log cabin sort of resort with little adorable kids who are thrilled to be at camp, and excited to learn archery, and at the end of every summer the counselors return to the city brown as berries, and glowing with summer memories, romances, and of course a load of loot they've saved, because Camp Kikishitshit has no stores, and is a zillion miles from civilization. So far at the end of every summer, after working at one of my superbly crappy summer jobs, the only things I have to show for my labor are ten extra pounds five of them on my ass, and a whole new crop of freckles. I actually have some in my ears now, how does that happen? I'm waiting for the day that all my freckles connect and then I'll look totally ethnic.

I often wondered who you had to know to get a camp counselor job? How young do you need to be when you first start applying for those jobs, 3 years old? I'm pretty sure they have standards in terms of who gets hired. For example, your name should probably be something you can short form like to names like Mo, JoJo, Tab, Tad, or something other shitey, waspy name. My name, Siobhan, is pronounced 'Shevaan' which is often shortformed to 'Shiv'. Not even in the same ball-park as JoJo, Mandy or Muffy. Also, most of the guys and gals who get my dream job as a camp counselor are athletic, toned and energetic. I, on the other hand, am 'rubinesque', according to my dad who thinks I'm beautiful the way I am, and totally not athletic. I have flame red hair and freckles on my freckles. Toned and tanned I will never be. On a humid day my hair grows to crinkly proportions, and more often than not, resembles a bright red pyramid perched on my head. The only thing that can control my unruly mass of hair is a hat. Unfortunately, finding a hat that can cover both my gigantic head of hair and my rather large head, Mom says I could easily carry ten pounds of spuds in my hat, is difficult, and so if it's really sweaty and humid I don a sort of Bob Marley type hat. Of course that hat was made to cover an acre of dreadlocks, and not a frizzy mass of crinkly ginger hair.

I know I will never get a camp counselor job, and if I'm honest I don't really care anymore. My mom always says the right thing for me is waiting just around the corner. Which friggin' corner is what I want to know? She never mentions the corner, the street name or even the town or city where this big deal corner is located. She also never mentions what the hell the 'right thing' is. I guess she says stuff like that to make me feel better, which doesn't actually do the job but that's okay, I feel okay anyway.

I have decided that this year was going to be different. It was going to be the year I would land the perfect job, the be all, end all of fabulous summer jobs. A job that will pay me a pantload of cashola, be fabulously exciting, and the experience I would gain from said fabulous job, would be a massively, massive addition to my resume someday. My bestie Marci and I began my search earlier than normal this year, she asked her folks, relatives and friends of friends for any leads. The two of us made lists of companies that could be looking for summer help. I was going to win and that was all there was to it. Marcie was pretty much set as far as summer jobs go, every year she works with her folks. I'm not sure that's a good thing, but it never seems to bother Marcie. She pretty much roles with the punches when it comes to summer employment. Can't say as I blame her, it's a job for two months not a career for life.

To reach my goal of job perfection, I created a killer resume that included character references from neighbors and friends as well as an essay outlining what the depth of my commitment would be to my employer. I scoured the newspapers, hit the job boards on the internet, and checked the bulletin boards at school for job openings, but I only managed to get one job interview that had any sort of potential. Of course, my luck, on the day of my interview the weather is hot and sticky, so in order to keep my friggin' bushel hair under house arrest I had to apply a half a pound of heavy duty hair control product all over it, before I even think of leaving the house. I put on a pair of my best navy pants, the only ones that don't make my butt look like I'm carrying a one year old child on my ass. I chose and carefully pressed a cotton shirt, a pair of espadrilles and a handbag. I spent quite a bit of time getting ready. I figured the job was worth a little extra effort. I started by carefully applying my makeup. I don't normally wear much makeup because I have never gotten the hang of putting it on so it looks natural. Which begs the question, why start now? Did I suddenly wake up with the knowledge of what it takes to apply natural looking makeup? The answer is no, but the lack of knowledge did not stop me from applying a touch more eye shadow and blusher than needed, and a shade of lipstick than even a clown would think twice about wearing. Just before I leave I applied an additional roll of deodorant, so I don't get sweat marks going down to my waist by the time I get to my interview.

I arrive at the interview location to discover ten other girls in the room, waiting to be interviewed for what I assumed to be the same job. As I look around the reception room it occurs to me that I am definitely the dark horse. The other girls are poised and relaxed, as if they couldn't care less if they got the job or not. Plus they all have shiny perfect hair, a freckleless complexion and perfectly put together outfits. I on the other hand have begun to sweat like a pig, and decide that I had better check myself out before they call my name for my interview. I ask where the women's washroom is, and after following the directions given by the miserable old trout behind the desk, I walk off to repair whatever damages the heat and my nerves have done.

One look in the mirror and my worst fears are realized. I notice that my larded down hair had begun to break free from the constraints of the styling gel that I had applied. After digging through my bag I manage to find a scrungie, and wrangle my hair into a bun. I next take a look at my face and realize that my mascara has suffered heat exhaustion, and moved halfway down my cheeks. After wiping off the offending black smear I move onto my eyeshadow, an unfortunate shade of blue, which looked dreamy in my inadequately lit bathroom, but now glows like a fishing lures across the lids of my eyes. I remove the lion share of my eyeshadow, touch up my lipstick, which looks like an angry gash of red on my lips, I thought it was a peach color when I bought it. After several minutes working over my whole look, I step back from the mirror and tweak my new hairdo and notice that my anti-perspirant has failed me miserably, and the ensuing sweat has reached the waistband of my pants. I went to the hand dryer and flipped up the nozzle, and held my armpit over the blast of hot air, hoping to dry out the offending sweat stains. Of course, while I'm doing that the heat from the dryer attacks my hair, creating dried out, fly-away tendrils and spikes of hair that sticking out all over my head like sprouting grass, and my face, because of the heat of the dryer is covered in a film of sweat. I looked like I'd been scrubbing toilets in the sweltering heat for hours.

After doing the best I could to spiff myself up, I headed back to the waiting room and found it was completely empty. Even the old crone behind the desk was gone. I yelled "hello, hello, anyone here" then I decided to sit and wait for someone to appear or call my name for the interview. After waiting for about twenty minutes I realized that I had spent so long in the bathroom that I missed my interview completely.

I left the building and walked down the street feeling completely defeated, and so pissed off I could have spit. There was nothing left to do but find a café, and toss another five hundred calories onto my ass. It just so happens that I am in a pretty posh part of town so there is an incredible number of chi places of indulgence to choose from. I settle on a bakery café place that looks like it won't cost a fortune to indulge in piece of 'poor me' chocolate cake.

I walk up to the counter where several other people are pointing to their choices, and nodding their approval when the baked delight is presented. Next to me is an older woman, I say older rather than old because it was hard to pinpoint the extent of her oldness, if you know what I mean. She was dressed in a coppery colored suit, her arms were full of gold bangles, and around her neck was a heavy, and no doubt real gold chain. She had gold hoops in her ears and a set of diamonds on her fingers, one ring was the size of a fresh ice cube, I swear. She smelled glorious, and when she spoke her voice had a sort of mid-Atlantic English accent sound about it. Her face was almost lineless, but her neck and hands gave away her age. I guessed her age to be at least seventy, but that's really a major guess because I had no clue. She put in her order, and after being handed it, she turned, and dropped it on the floor. She let out a little squeal, and she bent down to retrieve the mess and I stepped in front of her and said, 'you go and sit down while I look after this'. I don't have a clue why I did that, I'm not normally a Girl Scout, but something came over me. I didn't want her to stoop and have to clean up a mess, although the café immediately stepped into the breach to do the cleaning up. She turned to thank me and then walked toward a table. I picked up her new order, and my own and brought hers to her table.

"Thank you my dear, I appreciate your help so much" she said as I put down her drink and tart. "No problem, I hope you didn't get any on you," I said. "Please, won't you join me, I hate to sit alone in a restaurant, and you've been so helpful." Normally I would have said no, that I had places to go, and things to do, blah, blah, blah, but this time I said, "Thank you, I don't like sitting alone either." Yikes, what was going on, I was acting totally opposite to my usual obnoxious persona.

Her name was Natasha Romanoff. I had a hard time believing that it was her real name. Who has a name like Natasha? Isn't Natasha a villain in a Rocky and Bullwinkle cartoon? Over the course of the next hour or so, we talked about everything, she was totally interesting and not the least old lady like, if you know what I mean. I told her about my thwarted job interview, and my quest to find the best job I could possibly find for the summer. She laughed pretty hard when I described my attempts at tidying up. We kept on talking for a few more minutes, and then Natasha went quiet for a minute or so, and then she said, "I have a job for you if you would like. You're a smart young woman, articulate, and most of all kind and decent. I need an assistant. I am the chair of several charities, and run several small businesses and could use someone to help keep me organized," she said. I must have looked like a complete moron, staring at her with my mouth open like idiot, "You have a job, and you would be interested in hiring me? Oh wow, I would love it." I realized I sounded totally like a Pollyanna, and completely nauseating but I didn't care, I couldn't stop gushing, she had offered me a job, probably a good one and I seemed to have lost control of my cool girl facilities. "My dear Siobhan, you are exactly the kind of person I need to help me, and I would be delighted to work with you." She handed me her card and we arranged for me to show up at her place the following Monday. After a few more minutes we both stood up, and walked to the door. She turned and hugged me, and gave me a kiss on both cheeks, and then walked up to a big limo that was waiting for her at the curb. I just stood like a friggin' statute, with my mouth hanging open catching flies, and then waved to her as she climbed into her car.

I walked home, fifteen blocks, which is a long way for me, and I don't think my feet touched the ground; I was truly on cloud nine, all floaty and feeling awesome. I couldn't believe the day, and whole chain of events that culminated in my landing a dream job, with enough money to get my college fund up and running and some left so I could have a completely awesome time this summer. I was swimming in joy. I got home and told my folks the whole story, not leaving out one single detail. My Mom nearly peed her pants laughing at the story of myself in the bathroom, and Dad sat nodding his head, saying he knew all along someone would discover how great I was. Yeah, my folks are pretty wonderful.

It's Thursday, and I had a weekend plus a day to get ready for my new job. Normally, the old Siobhan, would spend the weekend hanging around with my friends, eating crap and laying around doing zip. With my job all sorted out I decided to give myself a makeover. Hair, makeup, manicure, pedicure, shave my legs, pits and a facial, the whole body deal. I also decided to do a cleanse that would hopefully knock off a few pounds before my Monday morning job start. I began the cleanse on Friday. I spent the day drinking copious amounts of warm water with lemon for sustenance. By six o'clock in the evening I was so hungry I could easily have gnawed my own arm off. Eventually I weakened and scarfed down a peanut butter sandwich and chased it down with a jug of chocolate milk. Remorseful, I took two laxatives and went to bed. Right after I swallowed the laxatives I said to myself 'why did you do that?" but it was way too late. Rationalizing, I thought to myself, maybe the laxatives will help me drop a couple of pounds before Monday. Saturday morning I woke up like a shot, raced to the bathroom, and spend the next two hours wishing I hadn't given mother-nature a nudge. What a jerk I am sometimes.

Monday morning rolled around, and I got up at the crack of dawn to get ready for my first day of work. I planned on bringing my own lunch to cut down on expenses, so after getting dressed in a pair of dress pants, and a shirt I hit the kitchen to make my sack lunch. Mom beat me to it, and made me a lunch of gargantuan proportions. When I commented that it is a meal for one and not an infantry, she reminded me that I'll be working hard, and so if I need a snack later in the day, I need only dive into the grocery bag of food she's packed for me to find some sort of nutritional sustenance. I didn't have time to edit the bag, or argue so I took it, and headed out of the house. Just as I turned to close the door, a stretch limo pulls up in front of the house, and before I can even question its appearance, the driver jumps out, and opens the passenger door and gestures me inside. Of course, I look around thinking there has to be someone behind me he is gesturing to. Just as I turn back Natasha pops her head out and waves me inside. The only thing I can think is wow, wow and total wow. I had no idea how she knew where I lived. I had told her all about myself, but for the life of me I didn't remember give her my address. Maybe I did give it to her. I was talking a mile a minute after she offered me a job. I shudder to think what else I told her. It's all a total blank to me now.

"Hi Siobhan, get in we're going to do some shopping, before we go to the office," she said and I said, to myself of course, why the heck not. In the course of the morning we stopped at a bakery, a butcher, flower shop and vegetable market. We then stopped for a cold drink at a beautiful little outdoor café. "I should have mentioned, Monday is my shopping day. I like to shop for food for the week, and then in the afternoon, spend a couple of hours at Neiman Marcus and Saks. I hope you don't mind?" Natasha asked. "Are you kidding this a great way to start a new job."

Our next stop was Neiman Marcus and its hotsy, totsy fashion floor, not a place I frequent, like ever. The women all seemed to know Natasha, and gushed over her like she was a movie star. Maybe she is or was. Maybe she's one of those older stars I don't know about, one who had a really famous life before she retired. She picks out a bunch of silk blouses, a jacket and a whole wack of shoes. She then has them bring a ton of bras and panty sets, garter belts, merry widows, her name not mine, and all kinds of other sexy underwear. I was feeling pretty uncomfortable because, I was looking at her and thinking whoa, when are you ever going to wear this kind of thing. Natasha looks at me and realizes that I'm a little taken aback. "Darling, these aren't for me. There for my girls, my employees." After she said that she started to laugh. I was sitting there thinking, what kind of boss buys her employees sexy underwear? Then I thought I hope she doesn't buy any of that stuff for her newest employee. Me. I'm happy wearing my orthopedic 100% cotton knickers in sensible white, and my easy to put on sports bra, thank you very much!

Finally after a morning and part of the afternoon indulging in some retail therapy we head back to what I'm thinking is the office. The car pulls up in front of this big ass brownstone and Lucius, the driver, opened the door and I climbed out followed by Natasha. Lucius is left to wrangle all of the parcels and bags from the trunk. I am holding my handbag, and my picnic bag of lunch. By this time it is now two o'clock and I'm so hungry I could eat the entire contents of the bag. "What do you have in the bag my dear?" Natasha asks. "It's my lunch." I answered, suddenly very self-conscious of the enormity of said lunch. "My goodness, are friends joining you?" Then she laughs and I say "No, but you're welcome to have some. I know it seems like a lot but my Mom was worried that I might be hungry later in the day, so she packed extra." "What a wonderful idea, you and I can enjoy your lunch together in the dining room."

I was dreading the contents of my packed lunch, hoping its cheese and ham on white bread with some fruit and carrot sticks or something like that, but I know Mom, and I'm pretty sure the bag housed ten meatloaf sandwiches, a few boiled eggs and at least fifteen homemade peanut butter cookies.

We walked into the house, and were greeted by a man dressed sort of like a butler in black trousers and a black vest with a white shirt that was so perfect it looked painted on, and an attitude to match his painted on white shirt. He took Natasha's bag and scarf, and I followed her to a room off the foyer. It's a medium size room, with a desk and a computer, and a shelf behind the desk with a printer and books and files. In front of the desk are a couple of chairs, and up against one wall is a leather sofa, two more chairs and a coffee table. "This will be your office Siobhan. I think everything you need is here. My office is right through that door." She points to the door and opens it. I follow her to the threshold and wait. "Come on in and sit down, let's have a chat then we'll have some of your wonderful lunch."

She headed to her desk and I took a seat in front of her desk. Her office was quite large and very beautiful. Completely paneled in a rich dark wood, with old paintings on the walls, probably by some famous artist of expensive proportions. The draperies were lush with dramatic colors of pinks, violet and burgundy, and the sofas and chairs were paisley prints and stripes in that matched everything else. The overall effect was really feminine looking, but totally professional. After a few minutes of talking about the morning, she handed me a sheet she had written to explain what my job entails. I was to look after her appointments, keeping them straight, type all her letters and help her out with her various charity commitments. Twice a day I was supposed to walk her two dogs Coco and Lola. I hadn't had the pleasure, but I assumed they were fluffy, yappy miniature dogs that could fit in my pocket. Yikes, was I ever wrong. She used her intercom to call her 'head up his ass' butler, and asked him to bring her darlings, Coco and Lola, up to meet their new sister. I wanted to puke at the reference, but instead I feigned excitement at meeting my new siblings. Shit I can be so nauseatingly phony at times. Five minutes later, a quick knock on the door and in came the 'darlings'. Two of the biggest, frigging Great Danes I've ever seen in my life. I want to yell, I'm not walking them without a saddle, but I kept that comment to myself. As big as they were, Coco and Lola turned out to be very well behaved, and if I may say, respectful of their older sister.

After meeting them the two of us went to the dining room to have lunch, and not a moment too soon, I was going to start sucking my hair if I had to wait any longer. The dining room was set with place mats, plates and cutlery as well as a coffee set. Natasha sat down, and I proceeded to unload the grocery bag of food. Sure enough meatloaf sandwiches and hard-boiled eggs are the blue plate special. "You don't have to eat it if you don't like meatloaf" I said, although my Mom's meatloaf is a culinary 'tour de force'. "Oh, meatloaf sandwiches, I haven't had one in years. I can hardly wait. Over the next half hour between inhaling sandwiches and eggs, coffee, peanut butter cookies, and sliced apples, we talk about everything from her charities to hair styles. It was one of the best lunches I've had in ages. Natasha wasn't 'old ladyish' at all, she was really cool.

After lunch we both went back to the office, and I familiarized myself with the computer, her phone system, and then typed a couple of letters for Natasha. At the end of the day she came out of her office and handed me a schedule for the rest of the week that included luncheons she was to attend, walk times for the two horses she calls her babies, and things she needed me to compile information on. Friday was penciled in as a reception day. Whatever that was, I was pretty sure I would find out.

When I got home that night I told my Mom and Dad about my day in finite detail. They were thrilled, and Mom set about preparing another picnic for the next day. I managed to stop her by explaining that Natasha would be out most of the day. A small white lie out of necessity never hurt anyone. Right?

The next morning I got up bright and early, and very excited about the day ahead. I put a pair of running shoes in my bag, for the dog walking part of my job. I was not looking forward to being dragged around the park by a pair of horses, but if that was the only rub about my dream job, then I'm a real 'horse walking' kind of gal.

When I got to the brownstone, I wasn't sure whether I should knock, because it's her house and her office, or just open the door and walk in. My question was answered because just as I reached the landing, the door opened, and a couple of beautiful young girls walked out the door. I watched them get to the sidewalk just as the limo pulled up and Lucius jumped out and opened the door for the girls. He saw me, and waved a 'good morning' sort of hello. I turned back to the door as 'Mr. Surly' was holding it open for me. By the look on his face I figured he must have just consumed his body weight in lemons. I breezed past him and headed toward the office.

"Good morning my dear. Get yourself a cup of coffee and come and join me." Two minutes later I am ensconced in a chair facing Natasha enjoying the dark delicious taste of French press coffee, so much better than the dark brown water I'm used to drinking. After about ten minutes of instructions and updates about the day ahead, I got up to leave taking my cup and Natasha's with me. There was a small kitchenette just off my office with a sink, microwave and fridge. I washed the cups, placed them in the rack, and returned to my desk, which had significantly more papers piled on it than the night before. At ten o'clock I went out to the foyer to track down the dogs to take them for their scheduled walk. I found both Coco and Lola patiently waiting by the front door. I was not looking forward to the dog-walking thing, but I grabbed their leads, and I am about to snap them on their collars when Natasha came out to the lobby. Let me explain about the whole dog-walking thing. One of the reasons for my discomfort, for lack of a better word, is the whole 'poop and scoop' deal. If the dogs were your average six pound terrier, wrapping my hand in a plastic bag, and hoisting the offending poop into a bag isn't all that daunting. But the two beasts I had to walk were a whole lot bigger, and that meant I was going to have to bring a shovel and a wheel barrel to scoop up Coco and Lola leavings. The thought of removing not one but two steaming piles of doggy doo left me feeling quite bilious, but I needn't have fretted, and lost sleep over it, which I did by the way. Natasha had someone assigned to stoop and scoop the poop, and that someone wasn't your truly. Thank the lord for that.

Teddy was Natasha's general dogsbody type guy, who did all the odd jobs around the place, including poop wrangling. Actually, now that I think about it 'dogsbody' is the perfect word to describe

Teddy, considering the dog poop scooping part of his job. I hoped that Teddy made a whacking great salary doing for Natasha and her ponies. After Natasha explained Teddy's involvement in the twice-daily walks, and the required distance the dogs should go in order to be properly exercised, Teddy the poop picker upper, and me step out into the morning sunshine. Teddy is armed with a small garden spade and a couple of garbage bags. He followed behind me for some reason, with his poop picking up gear in his hand ready to leap at the first squat Lola or Coco made. I actually thought he might try and catch their poop before it hit terra firma. I could have been wrong on that score, but he seemed like the kind of guy that would do something like that. He was like the guy in the parade that follows the elephants, scooping up after them along the parade route. After several discouraged attempts at some sort of conversation, I decided that Teddy can kiss my big fat flabby butt, and I focused on the task at hand, walking the dogs. The dogs, although pretty well trained, and well behaved, are incredibly difficult to control. They are big strong animals that seem to get along with each other, and therefore walk quite closely together. They had obviously walked the same route for quite a while, because they knew what was coming up next along the trail and seemed to get more and more excited. When we reached the entrance of the dog park, the off leash section, the dogs excitement had reach a fever pitch, and before I could disconnect them from their leads they were off in a full gallop. I had held onto them as long as I could, believing that my job was to keep them by my side, but I tripped, and went down still gripping the leads until I finally had to let them go. Snarly old Teddy was standing behind me with a smirk on his face. I wanted to turn around and drop kick the old creep, but instead I said, "You could have warned me. I nearly killed myself." "You never asked," he said and walked towards the now calmed down dogs, and readied his shovel as Lola empties herself on the grass. Of course, I'm silently laughing and thanking the entire deity of gods, that it isn't me picking up that gigantic mess of steaming crap. I secretly hoped that the two dogs had stored up a couple of days' worth of poop that they would unload for Teddy.

We got back to the house about an hour later, and I handed the dog's leashes over too 'Mr. Miserable', whom I will now refer to as Jenkins. I decided I couldn't continue to dream up new names that reflect his obnoxious attitude, he just wasn't all that interesting. Anyway after handing Jenkins the leashes I went to my office. Natasha was out for most of the afternoon but had left me several little notes written in her flowery scripty type handwriting. I worked without stopping until about one o'clock before realizing that I was hungry, so I got my lunch from the office fridge and took it back to my desk. I unwrapped my ham and cheese on whole wheat and dug in. While I'm eating my lunch and going over the document I am working on the office door opens, and a gorgeous looking model type, comes plowing through the door and heads to Natasha's office. "Excuse me can I help you? Natasha isn't in at the moment," I said. "Are you her new worker assistant or something? Never mind, it doesn't matter anyway, give Nats a message for me." I got out a writing pad and held a pen poised over the notepad waiting for her to give me the message. "Tell her not to book Mr. Sweaty Paws ever again. Got that, Mr. Sweaty Paws is not happening for me ever again." I'm writing out the message, without looking at her because I don't want her to go into any detail about Mr. Sweaty Paws. "Can you give me your name?" I ask. "Trust me, Nats knows who I am, but just so you know, it's Carolina." "Thanks Carolina, I'll make sure Natasha gets the message." Carolina gives me a tight little smile, and flounces out of the room, slamming the door as she exits. I watched as she left the room thinking, 'I really need to learn how to flounce.' Then I thought about my big ass swishing back and forth doing the 'flouncing' and realized me learning how to flounce was a bad idea.

Natasha finally returned about four o'clock followed by a very flamboyant looking thirty something guy, carrying fabric swatches and a laptop. "Hi Siobhan this is Felix he is redoing my salon. Come into my office at four thirty for a chat." I decided that Carolina's message about Mr. Sweaty Paws could wait until four thirty. At about twenty-seven minutes after four Natasha opened her office door and gently nudged Felix out the door. I looked over at her as she rolled her eyes, and then air kissed Felix, and sent him on his merry flamboyant way.

I stood up and followed Natasha back into her office. "Sorry about that, I have to put Felix on a time limit or he'll drone for ages about the importance of complimentary colors." "A girl named Carolina came into the office looking for you. She seemed a little upset, anyway I told her you were out and she left a message for you." I proceed to read the message she dictated about Mr. Sweaty Paws. Natasha, instead of smiling as I thought she would, turned pale, and told me that I could leave early. "I'll see you tomorrow dear." I decided to take the subway halfway home and then walk the rest of the way. I was beginning to feeI like something was going on at Natasha's that wasn't exactly normal or even above board. Mr. Sweaty Paws had some explaining to do, if you get my drift. By the time I got home, I had decided to do some discreet checking around the office, nothing heavy-duty or anything like that, just a little exploring when Natasha is out. I also decided I would talk to my best friend Marcy and see what she thinks. Marcy was totally cool and really level headed about everything.

Chapter 2

After I had dinner I met Marcy at a little coffee shop around the corner from my house. I had told Marcy about my job when I first got it, but I hadn't filled her on my first couple of days so I had a lot of ground to cover to bring Marcy up to speed. I walked into the café, and spotted her over in the corner. I had told her to bring her laptop so we can do a quick search on Natasha, and also check out some of her charities. I know it seems underhanded, but everyone does it, and besides I could be working for white slavers or a drug cartel and not know it.

"Hi Shiv, after I finish doing your sleuthing you have to tell me all about the first few days on the job." Marcy is such a character. She has a huge imagination, and loves drama and excitement more than just about anything else. When I told her we should get together and do a quick check on Natasha, I had to make her promise not to jump the gun and do anything before I meet her. "Hi Marc, are you all set up? Let's order some coffee and desserts and then I'll tell you everything." Over the next half hour I told her about the dogs, the limo, Jenkins, the Friday reception and finished my narrative with the Carolina, Mr. Sweaty Paws story. Marcy was completely silent and totally enthralled. I have to say my story telling style is quite incredible, dramatic at the right moments, subtle at others, definitely enthralling. "Whoa, what do you think of the Carolina babe? Was she like a hooker or just a piece of fluff? What'd your boss say when you told her," Marcy asked. "That's the thing, Natasha is usually really cool, but when I gave her the message from Carolina, she turned really pale, then sent me home early. I have a feeling something is going on at the office that's not totally kosher. Oh yeah, and Carolina was kind of slutty in a way, but not really if you know what I mean. She was totally not me or you, that's for sure."

Marcy Googled Natasha but only got a run down on all her charities. There wasn't anything about her past and almost nothing about her personal life. I still didn't know whether she was ever married, had any kids or whether her real name was Natasha Romanoff. After talking for another hour or so Marcy said, "I think I'm going to ask my Uncle Frank if he can find out something about Natasha Romanoff. Give me the address and stuff like that, and he can dig around and find out whatever there is about the house and Natasha." "Your Uncle Frank the cop? Would he get in trouble checking this kind of stuff out?" I asked. "He might if he got caught, but he won't get caught, and besides he loves a mystery, and this sort of thing is right up his alley. She could be a drug dealer or something like that. He'd be a hero if he dug up the goods on a big time drug dealer." "Yeah, I suppose he would, but then I'd be out of the best summer job I have ever had, and would have to go back to working at some Slurp and Burp." We got up and left the café. I told her I'd call her the next night and let her know if I'd found anything out. As we parted I said, "When you tell your Uncle Frank, don't let on its anything more than idle curiosity on my part, okay." "Don't worry I'll tell him that it's me that's interested in Natasha and her business," she said.

I got home in time to watch some TV with my parents, chew the fat about family junk, and then head off to bed. I hadn't told them anything about the job except that I really liked it, which I did, by the way.

The next day just as I stepped out the door I looked up and Natasha's limo was once again, parked in front of the house. Lucius climbed out, waved, and opened the door for me. "Hi Lucius, what are you doing here?" I said as I climbed into the back seat. "We're meeting Madam at Saks, so she sent me to pick you up, take you to breakfast, then meet her there. I've picked up some coffee and bagels, and I thought we'd have lunch in the park. What do you think?" "Great I'd love it." I said. Obviously, neither he nor Natasha knew the morning ritual at my house. A bagel and cream cheese is a breakfast appetizer in the Murphy household. My Mom believes in big breakfasts, and her and Dad get up extra early so they can get a head start on the breakfast buffet my Mom cooks every morning.

We drove to the park close to Natasha's brownstone, the same park I go to walk the beasts, and after we parked the car, Lucius brought out a picnic hamper, and the two of us found a bench and sat down with the hamper positioned between us. The two of us drank our coffee and I nibbled on the bagel, I ate so much breakfast before I left the house, anything more than a nibble would make me toss.

After breakfast we both sat sipping our coffee and then I asked Lucius "How long have you worked for Natasha?" "Let's see it's coming up for thirty-five years, at least" he said. I can't believe it, "Wow, that's a long time. Have you always been her driver?" "Always." "Is Natasha married?" I ask trying to sound casual not questioning. "Not anymore." I realized I shouldn't ask any more questions because the answers he was giving were becoming less and less enthusiastic. 'Always' and 'not anymore', 'soon' and 'maybe' are the type of answers I was getting to the questions I asked, so I put a lid on my interrogation, and shortly after we left to continue our trip to Saks Fifth Avenue. He dropped me off and said,

"Natasha said you know where to go. I'll pick both of you up in about an hour." I went up to the fashion floor and spotted Natasha surrounded by sales associates. "Ah Siobhan, come over tell me what you think." I walked over, and one of the girls rolled out a rack of beautiful cocktail dresses.

"I love them all. But if I was choosing one of them it would be the green silk dress," I said pointing to the most beautiful dress I had ever seen. "Go on then, try it on." Natasha said. "No, I couldn't, it's way over any budget I would ever have, and I might wreck it trying it on," I said. While I'm saying this Natasha nods, and the sales associate takes the dress of the rack, and walks it to the dressing room area. "No arguments. Let's see how you look, go on try it on, it won't bite you," Natasha said. I reluctantly agreed and walked to the dressing room like I was being punished for something. I am such a friggin' drama queen.

I'm in the dressing room, which by the way is the same size as my parent's living room. I got undressed, and then took the green beauty off the hanger, slipped it over my head and zipped it up. I turn around to face the mirror, and I can't believe what's looking back at me. I'm hot! Usually, when I try anything on, my first reaction is 'wow it fits me' and 'it's on sale' or 'it's dirt cheap'. How an outfit actually looks on me is way down on my list of shopping priorities. This dress looked incredible. There was a bunch of high heels in the room and I slipped my size tens into a pair, and stood back again to take a final look. Two seconds later a knock came on the door and I yelled "coming" as Natasha opened the door. "Oh my, you look beautiful. Of course I knew you would. Turn around and let me see the back." I spun around and gave Natasha an exaggerated pose. "Perfection, we're taking it," she said. "Oh no, we can't, it's way too much for my budget. I'm saving for college, I can't spend my money on a dress like this," I said. "Get changed, and I'll see you in a minute," Natasha said. I quickly got out of the dress, hung it up, and put my clothes back on. I brought the dress with me out of the dressing room, and handed it to the sales associate. Natasha was talking to the manager, and so I picked up the packages that she had already purchased, and told her I would take them down to the car.

After handing the bags to Lucius, I waited for Natasha. A few minutes later she came through the door with a couple of more bags, and after handing the bags to Lucius, we got in the car and headed for the office. When we arrived Coco and Lola were waiting for their walk. They were both standing quietly by my desk with their leashes hanging from their mouths, if they weren't so massively massive, they'd be cute. I dumped off my purse, took their leads, and the three of us left the office and walked towards the park. Of course, the dog shit wrangler followed a discreet distance behind us. After being dragged around the dog park for half hour or so, we returned to the office, and I went to my desk and reviewed my job list for the day.

About one o'clock I decided to take a break and go to the park to eat my lunch. I stuck my head through Natasha's door to tell her I was going to the park and would be back in twenty minutes. "Take your time dear."

I got to the park and called Marcy. "I'm going to do a little snooping this afternoon. Natasha has appointments and won't be around the rest of the day. Have you heard anything from your uncle?" I asked. "Not a thing he said the only thing he got from his search was her charities. He suggested checking the library for information, or the tax roll, whatever that is, to find out about the house she lives in." "I think she lives in the building where the office is, but I don't know for sure. I wonder if she owns the brownstone, if she does it's got to be worth a load of money. I'm planning on going through some of the files this afternoon. I want to find out whether she has any kids, and who she was married to. I also want to find out more about her employees. Lucius, her driver, is a nice guy but I think he's a bit slippery. Not that I know a lot about slipperiness, but there's something about him." We talked for a few more minutes, and then I rang off and headed back to the office.

I walked into my office, and there, hanging behind my chair, was the beautiful dress I had tried on earlier at Saks. I walked up to the dress, took it off the hook, and noticed a note pinned to the hanger. I opened the note "Siobhan this is for you. Wear it on Friday for the reception. No arguments. There is also a pair of shoes and an evening bag. You looked beautiful in it. Enjoy." I stared at the note, reading it again several times then I took the dress off the hanger, and held it up to myself. I was so happy, and overwhelmed with her kindness I wanted to cry. I hung up the dress again and sat behind my desk. I sat thinking about what a real creep I was for wanting to dig some dirt on Natasha. Was I nuts? Natasha was a wonderful woman, who gave me an incredible job, and she just bought me a zillion dollar cocktail dress, that I would never, ever, ever be able to buy for myself. She has shown me nothing but kindness and respect, and I'm about to snoop around her office looking for secrets. What a total jackass I am.

I worked quickly to get caught up on all of Natasha's correspondence and scheduling. I had decided that, although she had been really good to me, and I was acting like an ungrateful bitch, I still needed to know about her and her company. What can I say? I'm a drip and a meathead. I went through the computer files first to see if I could find anything of interest. There was file after file of correspondence, spreadsheets and calendars, but nothing personal. Her previous assistant kept everything very well organized and it was easy to search for files. I started looking for personal files and correspondence but soon realized that there was very little on the computer but business information. There were several leather boxes filled with files stacked on the shelves, stored by date and year. Many of the boxes went back several years. I started with the latest box, I didn't want to get caught snooping, so I removed some of the files and, returned the box to its spot on the shelf.

The box contained paper correspondence, and a DVD with the date written on the paper sleeve. I decided to take the DVD home with me and check it out on my laptop, and just read the papers. I scanned them quickly and all I found was schedules and letters. Nothing controversial, at least that I could see, to be honest I wouldn't know 'controversial' if it jumped up and bit me in the ass. After returning the papers to the box, I checked my watch, and realized it was past six. I called my mom and told her I was running late. I grabbed my new dress and shoes and hung them in the closet. I figured if I were going to wear them on Friday, I would change at the office. It's not like I wanted to bus to work on Friday in a cocktail dress, heels and a shopping bag full of meatloaf sandwiches.

By the time I got home my folks were in the living room watching TV. They eat their dinner every night at exactly six o'clock. The only time they deviate from their six o'clock chow down is if they have some sort of special event to attend, or are going out for the evening with some friends. "Hi dear, your dinner is in the oven keeping warm," my mom called from the living room. I went to my room and to change into sweats and my flip-flops, you've got to wear comfy clothes when partaking of my mom's nightly food fest. When I got back to the kitchen both my folks were waiting for me, there was a four minute commercial break going on, "So what's with the limo again this morning?" Dad asked. "I explained about the shopping trip, and the breakfast in the park. "Why didn't you invite this Lucius character to join us for breakfast, we always have lots," Mom asked. I told them I didn't really didn't know him all that well, and anyway I didn't know about the breakfast thing until I got in the car, and Lucius told me.

I told them all about the dress, and how Natasha had bought it for me. My mom was excited to see the dress but Dad was a little suspicious, he doesn't like being beholden to anyone. "What does she want you to do at this Friday reception?" he asked. "Come one Dad, I'm just a flunky greeter, I'm sure it's nothing sinister or kinky. She knew I didn't have any real special clothes that I could wear, so she bought me the dress." "You could have worn your bridesmaid dress from your cousin Connie's wedding. It looked beautiful on you," Mom said. The dress my mom was referring to was probably one of the universe's ugliest bridesmaid's dresses. It's certainly the nastiest looking dress I've ever seen or worn, and I've worn my fair share of ugly bridesmaid's dresses. I looked like a gigantic cupcake in it. It had big puffy sleeves, a bow in the front that spanned the width of my chest and another bow of equal gigantic proportions slapped above my ass on the back. The worst thing about the dress was the unfortunate color 'lilac', with purple trim. I would rather have gone naked than wear that dress. Of course I didn't say that to Mom, or Connie for that matter. I'm so syrupy nice sometimes, I almost make myself sick.

After cleaning off my plate and putting it in the dishwasher I went upstairs to my room. I switched on my computer and then slid the DVD into the drive. It contained about fifty files. I opened each file, and found excel files that contained spreadsheets of numbers and dates. Each excel file had a number as its name. There were about ten different number names. The numbers and files made no sense to me, but I copied the whole disk onto my hard drive, and put the original back in my purse after wiping it clean of fingerprints; I watch way too much CSI stuff, but a gal can never be too careful.

When I got to work the next day I put my bag down, and went in to thank Natasha for my dress. Horror of horrors the file I had looked through the night before was sitting on her desk. "Hi Siobhan, how are you this beautiful morning?" "Wonderful! I wanted to thank you for my dress. I don't know how I can ever pay you back for you generosity." "Nonsense, you looked wonderful in it, and you needed it for your job. Consider it a uniform. However, if you want to pay me back by bringing some of your Mom's meatloaf sandwiches to work every so often that would suit me just fine. They're worth a dozen dresses easily." I smiled big time and went back to my office. I was feeling like such a turncoat I had decided not to sniff around anymore. What did it matter anyway? What was I hoping to find out? Now my only problem was hiding the DVD I had taken home, so that it looked like it just fell out of the box or something.

By the end of the day I had taken the dogs for another quick gallop around the park, finished off all the correspondence I had on my desk, and then Natasha and me sat down and went over the food, drinks and flowers for the Friday reception.

When I got home that night I called Marcy and told her about the DVD thing, and everything else that had happened. "I can totally understand how you feel. I called my uncle and he said he still hadn't found anything, but suggested we find out more about her driver Lucius." We talked for about a half hour. I told her about my dress and, of course, Marcy was dying to see it.

The next day went by pretty quickly. I had to supervise the rental guys, making sure they arranged the tables in the right spots around the reception room. I hadn't seen that part of the house yet, and it was beautiful. The main room was really big, and led to a big solarium type room with a terrace off of it. There were lanterns and lights that needed to be strung up around the terrace, as well as planters to arrange and table linens to put on all of the tables. By the time we were finished the whole place looked like fantastic. It was almost like I had a clue what I was doing. Go figure. Natasha came in at the end of the day, and she was very happy with the results. "Perfection my dear Siobhan. Everything is enchanting." Oh I am so good I can't stand it!

I went home, and after dinner I went to my room, and by nine o'clock I was in bed and fast asleep. I had told Natasha I would be at the office by seven in the morning and I didn't want to be late.

Chapter 3

When I arrived at the brownstone the next morning there was a flurry of activity everywhere. Hairdressers and make-up artists had set up work stations in my office. There was a rack of party dresses in Natasha's office, and people bustling around everywhere. I was standing by my desk trying to figure out what was going on when Natasha burst through the door followed by five, twenty something girls. I stood watching the chaos ensue, and I'm pretty sure my mouth was hanging open. The girls poured over the dresses, pulling out their favorites to try on, which they managed to do in seconds, peeling off their clothes, and stepping into their chosen dress. Clearly, modesty wasn't a big deal to them. I don't suppose it would be a big deal to me either if I had a body like those girls. Thongs and push up bras were quickly covered with sequins and satin, in a rainbow of colors. After the flurry of trying on dresses the group of girls were in their chosen dresses, and Natasha walked into the room to see the girls. After a quick once over by Natasha, they changed back into their regular clothes, and left the office to go for lunch. I was still dumb struck, but I was now seated at my desk staring at my computer screen, waiting for an explanation to pop up on the screen, or something. As if.

I took the dogs for their walk, and decided to give Marcy a call while I was out. I told her what went on that morning, and she had no logical explanation either. By the time I got back and had my lunch, the girls had started to come in for their hair and makeup. It was like we were hosting a fashion show, instead of a business reception.

I went to check on the reception room, supervise the caterers, and help with the bar set up. The reception was scheduled to begin at six o'clock. I still didn't get what the girls were for, and I was getting a weird vibe about the whole evening. Actually I was getting more than a weird vibe, I was a bit freaked out. I didn't have a clue what the reception was in aid of. If it was a charity event what were the bevy of babes in aid of? Once the girls were finished with their hair and makeup Natasha sat and had her hair done.

At about five o'clock I went to tell Natasha that I was going to get ready. "Not until your hair and makeup are done." Natasha said. "Oh, it's okay I can do my own. But thank you anyway," I said. Natasha came over to me and took me by the hand and guided me to the chair. "No, you absolutely must have your hair and makeup done, it will complete your look. Franco, do your magic. No arguments Siobhan, sit back and enjoy." She swished out of the room yelling, "I'll be in my room changing."

Over the next forty-five minutes I watched as Franco and his team transformed my unruly, red wire-like hair into big soft curls, and applied my makeup so subtly, that it didn't look like I was wearing any at all. "Ooh la la, you look marvelous. You are a big, beautiful girl, and I Franco have turned your face and hair into utter perfection." I looked at myself in the mirror after he had finished and I couldn't believe my eyes, I looked like someone else. Like I'd borrowed a face for a night. I wished Marcy could see it. I got my cell phone out and took a selfie of my transformation and sent it to Marcy. I looked super good and super-hot. I put on my dress, my shoes, picked up my little evening bag and went out to the reception room.

Natasha came up to me when I walked in the room, "Oh my, you look like a real beauty. Of course, I knew you would with your wonderful hair, and your peaches and cream complexion. Stunning!" I thought 'peaches and cream' she obviously didn't notice my record breaking collection of freckles. "Oh thank you, I feel so beautiful. What do you want me to do? Where do you want me to stand?" I asked. "Just stand by the doors, and greet our guests as they arrive. Keep an eye on the waiters, make sure they're circulating around, and just look gorgeous."

I positioned myself at the door, and a few minutes later the guests began to arrive. All of them were men ranging in age from about thirty to eighty years old. The girls were all standing around talking as the men came in. One old geezer asked me about myself, and when I was available, and when I told him I worked for Natasha as her assistant, he stomped off, and headed for one of the other girls in the room. Figures the only guy to approach me, not that I wanted anyone approaching, was an old boot well passed his sell-by date. I did wonder why he asked me when I was available, but I was so preoccupied I didn't let it bug me. I figured I would find out eventually.

Over the course of the evening, more women turned up all dressed to the nines, some of them a little older than the ones that were trying on dresses in Natasha's office. I was beginning to feel a bit uncomfortable with the whole reception. It looked like a singles club mixer, not a fancy assed reception. I decided that come Monday I was going to ask Natasha straight out, what the reception was in aid of, and if she fired me, so be it. I had also decided that I would start snooping again. Something was going on, and I planned on finding out what that something was, although I'm not sure why I was so focused on finding out. I guess I'm just a naturally nosy jerk. Maybe Natasha was a Madam. OMG if that was the case, I could be charged with some sort of criminal behavior. I wasn't sure what that charge would be, but you never know. Maybe they would think that I was a hooker or something as well. I was standing at the door decked out in a flashy looking dress, so I could easily have been some sort of classy type hooker. Listen to me 'classy hooker', I'm a high school student working at my dream summer job.

I had visions of being taken out of the brownstone in handcuffs, while hundreds of paparazzi snapped pictures of me. The pictures would be all over the tabloids and my life would be ruined. Perhaps a little dramatic, but I still had to find out what was going on. If Natasha fires me, I'll be back working at some Slurp and Burp by next week.

By ten o'clock most everyone was gone and the reception, or whatever you call it was winding down. Natasha came up to me and said "I guess you have a few questions about the evening, so why don't you and me have a sit down on Monday. Lucius will take you home. Thank you for all your help, and don't worry I'll explain it all on Monday." She then kissed me on the cheek and I rounded up by work clothes and went out to the waiting car.

In the midst of everything, I had forgotten I was still wearing my Cinderella cocktail dress. When I walked in the door my folks were waiting for me. "Oh my goodness, you look like a movie star. I knew you were beautiful, but wow," my Dad said. My Mom was totally speechless and went to get the camera. "I have to have pictures of you to send you grandmother. She will be thrilled." My grandmother is a bit crazy, I love her to bits, but she's a real wack-a-doodle fruitcake most of the time. She is as blind as a bat, and refuses to wear glasses except for reading. She crochets a Christmas vest for me every year and I am obliged to don said vest and wear it for the entire day. I don't need to describe it, suffice to say it has a definite holiday feel about it complete with holly, reindeers and bows. Besides her holiday craft products, she produces huge amounts of doily dresses for me during the year. I can't imagine wearing one of the dresses she makes. My granddaughter sweetness ends at actually wearing one, I won't even try one on. When I am handed a doily dress I tell Gran that I'm going to put it away and try it on when my hair and makeup are all done properly. She just nods and agrees with me saying, "You're right dear. Try it on when your hair and makeup are all done up and you'll be able to do justice to the dress." My thoughts exactly.

"Tell us all about the reception. Was it glamorous? I'm sure it was. Tell us all about it and don't leave out any details," Mom said. I had to choose my words carefully, and glaze over most of the goings on, saying that it was filled with a lot of important people. I described the food, flowers and music, and then feigned exhaustion and went up to my room. I took a long bath and then went to bed. My brain had been in overdrive all night and it was about to shut down completely.

Saturday night my friends and me were going to a club, so Marcy came over early so I could tell her about the event. Before we started, I showed her the dress and shoes and some more pictures of me all decked out including a couple of close ups on my makeup and hair. "Totally wow. You looked amazing. Your hair and makeup are incredible, and that dress is to die for. You looked like a movie star." After holding up the dress to herself in the mirror, and slipping her size seven feet into my size ten boats, we sat on the bed and I told her all the details, leaving out nothing. By the time I had finished Marcy was sitting totally silent. "She said she would talk to you Monday. Yikes, I wonder what she's going to say?" I wondered that as well. What could the evening have possibly been in aid of?

Marcy and I met our friends in the club, and spent rest the night having a great time, and not once did I think about Natasha and her gang.

All day Sunday I laid around the house worrying my butt off about Monday. To say I was a bit nervous by the time Monday morning rolled around was putting it mildly. I could be out of a job by ten a.m., or become part of a sex for hire organization, and have criminal stamped on my forehead. Neither outcome appealed to me one little bit. I know I was being a tad dramatic, but that's me, I can't control the drama, it's like part of my DNA.

When I got to the office Natasha was already working away in her office. I stuck my head in to say good morning and she said "Good morning to you dear. Come to my office about ten for coffee, and we can have a chat." Great I'm thinking my timeframe was correct. Ten o'clock was the do or die hour. I was so distraught, that I had actually failed to consume massive quantities of breakfast and was feeling hungry. Most likely my hunger was triggered by nerves, yeah right, nerves my ass; my hunger can be triggered by anything from bus fumes to birds chirping.

At ten o'clock Lorna the domestic staff, or whatever she's called, opened the door and wheeled a coffee service into Natasha's office. A minute or so later Natasha rang me to join her. I walked into her office like I was headed for the gallows, and guess who was sitting on one of the side chairs, Lucius. I knew it! I knew he was more than a driver; he was her partner in crime, whatever the crime was. "Come in dear, take a seat. Let me get you a coffee." I sat down and Natasha handed me a cup of coffee. "I thought you might have some questions about last Friday's reception, and rather than have you speculate, I thought Lucius and I would tell you what we do here." I was a little uncomfortable. I didn't want Natasha to think that I was a dumb kid or anything like that. I said, "I sort of wondered what the reception was all about, but you don't have to explain anything to me. I'm cool with whatever it was about." "I know you are, and I also realize that you are a young girl, but I really like you as my assistant, and I want to be straight with you. If after I explain everything, you decide you don't want to work here anymore, I will understand," Natasha said. "I love working here, and no matter what it is, I want to stay." I said although in the back of my mind I was thinking, if she said she was a white slave trader, I don't know what I would have done. Well actually I do. I would have run like hell with my heals kicking my ass all the way home. Once home I would run up to my bedroom, close the door and put a chair up against it and crawl like a whimp under my bed.

"Don't worry Siobhan we aren't white slave traders, or anything like that," Natasha said. My eyes must have been as big as saucers, she had read my mind, "I don't think that at all," I said blinking so many times I made myself dizzy. Natasha looked at Lucius who up to that point hadn't even acknowledged me. He said, "We run an escort service, a very private and very discreet escort service." I sat completely still and Natasha continued, "The men that use our service are very well known business men, doctors, lawyers and politicians, who pay a lot of money to have good looking, intelligent women as escorts whenever they need one." I sat for a minute trying to keep my face neutral, it's not like they said they were a gang of thieves or anything like that. "You mean like a dating service?" Yes, I actually asked that dumb assed question. "Well not really, it's a escort service. The girls we have working for us are taught to be discreet, and not pursue long-term relationships with their clients. Usually the men ask for the same girl or type of girl as their escort. We strive to keep the dates as business like and professional as possible. We do not condone any hanky panky, it's not encouraged or tolerated. At the end of each engagement, the girls check in with us, and update us on the status of their client. They tell us how it went, and if he was satisfied, happy, unhappy or forward and inappropriate in any way," Natasha said. I sat for a couple of seconds taking it all in, and then I said, "Don't the men try it on sometimes? They could offer the girls money for a little extra service, that sort of thing." The two of them looked at me like I had said something outrageous, and I thought me and my gigantic gob have just blown it, instead Natasha said, "I knew you were a smart girl from the moment I met you. You're right, the men often try it on, and for the most part the girls tell us about it, and we deal with the gentleman in question either by refusing future service, or sending a new girl. That's not to say that it doesn't go on, but we do try our best to keep it all above board." "Suppose the police found out, couldn't you be in trouble. They could accuse you of running a brothel or being a Madam," I said. "You're right, I could be put in a very difficult position, however, that hasn't happened so far. We have a lot of extremely influential men as clients, and we feel certain we would be protected from prosecution," Lucius said.

I was sitting there listening to him thinking 'you mean you pay for protection'. The three of us sat silent for a minute or two then Natasha said, "Running an escort service that caters to rich and influential men helps us with our charities. Many of our girls are booked to work as product models at trade shows and conventions. One of the reasons we started the service was to get the connections we needed to raise money. The men that are our clients have no problem donating money, and endorsing any of our charities, and that is the biggest reason we do all this." Natasha said. "Do your clients endorse your charities because they don't want to get found out, or something like that?" I asked. "Good question. I'm not sure why they are eager to help. I like to think they believe in the charity and feel philanthropic, but you never know. Honestly I don't care. I have never given off the impression that they had to help out, there is no blackmailing even subtly," Natasha said.

Since Natasha and Lucius were being straight with me I decided to ask outright about their relationship, I know it's probably none of my stupid business, but I had to know. "Lucius and I used to be husband and wife. We were married for twenty years, but discovered we were better friends and business partners than marital partners. Please keep in mind our prior relationship is very private." "Oh don't worry, I won't tell anyone about anything. I didn't mean to pry. Chalk it up to my being very young and nosey," I said and I sort of meant it, but I was going to have to tell someone or would explode, so I needed to decide whether it was my parents or Marcy. If I told my parents, they could go one of two ways, either demand that I quit my job right away, or tell me that it was the most exciting job I could ever have, and keep my head down and enjoy the ride. I knew their reaction would be the former, not the latter scenario. I knew I would tell Marcy, but first I would swear her to complete and utter secrecy.

"Lucius and I have something we would like you to become involved in, something you can help us with, and don't worry we're not looking for another escort or anything like that. We would like you to befriend a couple of the girls that work for us. We aren't sure about them, and we think that a young girl like you could find out what, if anything is going on that shouldn't be going on. What do you think? Can you handle that? If you feel like it's too much, or you feel uncomfortable, we understand. We just thought you're young and they will relate to you pretty easily." It took me three seconds tops to answer, "I would be happy to help you, just tell me who the girls are, and stuff like that, and I'll figure out a plan to get close to them." Natasha and Lucius had big smiles their faces, and we finished our coffee in relative silence.

I went back to my office, and after checking e-mails, and sorting out my desk I went to get Lola and Coco for their morning 'drag Siobhan' session in the park.

By the time I got back to the office there was a couple of files on my desk. Each file contained a photo of a girl, and her background, including interests and education. The first girl was Georgette

Brownlee a really beautiful twenty three year old. She had a college education, and lived in a very good neighborhood. I figured she must share her living accommodations with a girlfriend because it was definitely not a cheap address. She liked riding, working out and cooking. Reading about her interests I knew right away we weren't ever going to be great buddies. I hate horses, working out, and I can't boil water, let alone cook. The second gal was Gina Prospero, and she was also a stunner, and her background seemed a little closer to mine. She lived in an average neighborhood, she liked the movies, swimming, and was taking stained glass classes. She had a couple of years of college, but dropped out because she couldn't afford the tuition. My kind of gal!

After I finished reading the files, and finishing off the work on my desk Natasha called me into her office. "I'm going to give you my girls' schedules just so you know what is going on. You don't need to do anything with them, but it's good for you to have them. Did you read the files I left for you?" "Yes I did, both of them seem like interesting girls. Georgette is a little out of my league in terms of background and interests, but I'll figure out some way of getting to know her. Gina sounds more like me in a lot of ways," I said. "I think you're probably right, but I'll leave most of it up to you. I have arranged for the girls to come in to see me in the next couple of days, so it will give you a chance to meet them, and make a connection, if you can."

On the way home my head was swimming with information and I felt a little bit uptight. A little bit! Who am I kidding I was a freaking wreck. I had spent the day trying to be cool with everything, but I wasn't cool with everything. I didn't understand the whole escort business. I thought it was pretty demeaning to the girls, and I wondered what kind of a-hole has to have a babe, that he paid for BTW, on his arm when he's out socially. I figured they were either pervs or total losers. Apparently some of them have wives, but prefer the company of a looker escort type bimbo when they go to certain types of events, rather than bring the old lady they married. I shouldn't call the girls bimbos, especially since I don't know them, but I gotta say I can't see me ever being an escort. The guy's different story, I don't need to know them to think that all of them are sleaze balls, as far as I'm concerned anyway.

When Natasha gave me the schedules I noticed that many of the agency clients were the city's rich and famous men. I understood what Natasha meant about her clients helping her raise money for her various charities. Not that I'm a total expert on the famous men of New York but I'd seen their names in the newspapers. Then I thought maybe she was a blackmailer, even though she had said no, she could be, you never know. The idea of Natasha being a blackmailer or involved in blackmailing made me gasp for air. Shitty shit, shit.

No doubt about it, I was up to my neck in the Natasha's agency. I had agreed to befriend two of her girls to find out if they are involved in any extracurricular hanky panky. I had been told, and must keep to myself, the fact that Lucius and Natasha are partners, and that they used to be husband and wife, and they might even be blackmailing their clients. I think that about covers it. I would soon discover that there was a whole lot more going on at the office than escorts.

When I got home my Mom had kept dinner for me in the oven. It was a massive platter of food, including half a meat pie, ten pounds of spuds and a garden of vegetables. Honestly, if I ate even a quarter of the food my Mom puts together and calls a meal, I'd be half a ton. I have tried to tell her that I just can't eat all the food she puts in front of me, but it's like she tunes out or doesn't listen or forgets. I don't know which it is, but the smorgasbord she calls dinner isn't getting any smaller.

After eating what I could, I cleaned up the kitchen and went up to my bedroom. My folks were over at the neighbor's playing cards, a weekly commitment that is still going strong after at least ten years. I called Marcy when I got to my room, and I told her I had something to tell her that had to be kept a complete and utter secret. After hearing the complete and utter secret thing, she said she'd be over in about an hour. I love Marcy, she is so transparent, she always sounds so adult and all that, but I know she loves the intrigue so much she could spit. I decided to take a shower and wash my hair before Marcy showed up. By the time she rang the doorbell I had showered and changed into sweats.

"Hi, come on in. Do you want some coffee?" I said as we walked to the kitchen. "Yes, for the coffee but hurry up, I want to hear all the poop, and if I don't hear it soon I'll grow a third leg waiting." When the coffee was ready I put the pot and mugs on a tray and we went to my room. "Before I tell you anything, you have to swear that anything I tell you is completely confidential. It's serious, and I can't let anyone find out, but I have to tell you, or I will seriously explode."

For the next hour I told her about my meeting with Natasha and Lucius, and then we rehashed it, and talked about what could happen if any of it got out. I told her I had seen some of the names on the client roster, and that some of them were some pretty big cheeses around town. I didn't tell Marcy any of the client's names; that would have been way too tempting for her. Not that Marcy is a big mouth, but having those names swirling around in her head could lead to a slip of the tongue at anytime. Nope telling Marcy the names would have definitely tempted fate big time.

"I'll keep you posted on what's going on, and if you have any good bonding ideas for me to use with those two girls, let me know." I walked her to the door and just as I was closing the door my folks came in. Of course, I had to tell them about my day, the edited version of my day, that is.

After filling my parents in about my swell but totally made up day, I went up to my room and switched on my computer. I had decided to spend some time seeing what I can find out about some of Natasha's charities. There were about ten different charities that were pretty active, and each of them had dedicated bank accounts. I managed to find nine of the ten charities on the internet, and they all seemed pretty legitimate. They were dedicated to good causes like clean water, education and medical supplies. Each of the charities was named after a state. Not terribly creative, but easy to remember, I suppose. The missing charity was going to be my challenge. It was called The Rhode Island Commemorative Charity. I continued my search for information until I got tired and went to bed. I was going to make finding out as much as I could about the Rhode Island Commemorative Charity a priority. Well maybe not a priority, but I'll give finding out about it a shot.

I got to work a bit early the next day, made the coffee, and then started my day. I had to write thank you letters to all of the donors for Natasha's last big fundraiser. I dug out a promotional piece on the event so I would have points of reference for dates and stuff, I also needed to read up on what the event was in aid of. I wrote a couple of different versions of a thank you note for Natasha to read and review. I also made a list of the people who were getting the thank you notes as well as tax receipts. Philanthropy with a big fat perk, I love it.

"These are great Siobhan, I would also like to add a memento to each package when we send them out. Let's you and I put our heads together and try and figure out something that would be an appropriate thank you gift." "I'll write up some ideas and give them to you. Is that okay?" I asked. "Perfect in the meantime I'll tweak these letters and we can start getting the packages ready to go out."

I returned to my desk and was working away when I felt someone looking at me. I looked up, and staring at me with their paws on the desk were Coco and Lola. They scared the crap out of me, I felt like they were looking at dinner. Anyway just as I looked up Natasha came into my office and just about passed out laughing. The dogs never moved a muscle. “I guess I’d better get their leashes. I’d hate to be late walking them,” I said and got up. Natasha laughed even harder. “You’re such a card Siobhan. Looks like my babies love you.” If slobbering all over me and jumping up and down around me means love, then yes they’re smitten. I know I have that effect on a lot of people, now I can include the animal kingdom on my list of conquests. Yeah right I am such a big A-hole.

After returning from their morning gallop I handed their leads over to Mr. Personality, Jenkins and went back to my office. I walked into Natasha’s office and asked her if she was around tomorrow for a lunch feast of veal sandwiches and red velvet sandwich cookies for dessert. “Are you kidding? I’d cancel lunch with the Mayor for veal sandwiches,” she said. I believe she would. My Mom makes legendary veal sandwiches.

I kept working on the thank you letters and tax receipts, and then made a list of gift ideas for Natasha to review. I have a good friend who is an incredible photographer and I thought we could choose a few of his photos and have them printed, framed and signed by him. Or we could commission him to photograph something exclusive to the charity. Another idea I had was including a day pass to Coney Island and a certificate for a Nathan’s hot dog, something different and unexpected. I also thought a seed pearl broach or pin with the charity name inscribed on it. The pin would be elegant and simple that could be worn by men and women. I thought the broach idea was good because we could use that type of gift for all the charities. I gave the list to Natasha and explained a bit about each idea. She loved them all and said we could discuss them tomorrow.

She had told me that Georgette was due in the office tomorrow. Natasha had told her she wanted to have a chat about a new client, so the plan was that I would spend time with her first, and say that Natasha was running a little late. While waiting for Natasha I could ask her if she wanted a coffee and then then two of us could bond or some crap like that.. "What kind of things should I talk to her about? I don't want to come across like I'm being nosy or anything like that," I said. "Just be yourself. You're so talented at putting people at ease, that it won't be a problem. Trust yourself and your ability. I will say this about Georgette she isn't a genius, even with a college education, so she's pretty easy to talk to," Natasha said. "If you think I'll be okay, then I'll do the best that I can."

Chapter 4

Marcy and I have signed up for a dance class. It's my homage to fitness and it's a hell of a lot better than running, which I couldn't or wouldn't ever do. As far as I'm concerned I've got way to much that could bounce around to do any sort of running. I haven't a clue what Zumba is all about, but I figure it's dancing, how hard can it be? Marcy said it was the latest dance and fitness craze, so the two of us are meeting a couple of other friends to start our first class. I changed into a pair of shorts and a t-shirt and grabbed my version of a gym bag, a plastic grocery bag with a water bottle a towel and a change of shoes.

Zumba, is a cross between dance and hard core aerobics. I had read all about it in a magazine and it sounded pretty cool, the hard core bit kind of scared me. It's supposed to be a real killer of a workout, and definitely way beyond my fitness level but I was game. Marcy is way more of an athlete than me, but an amateur compared to the rest of the participants in the gym. It looked like the Olympic village in there. Matchy, matchy outfits with sweat bands and perfectly toned bodies. Marcy and me positioned ourselves at the back of the class, and after listening to the instructor go over the days dancing plans and putting up our hands to acknowledge that we were newbies, the music began. Were they kidding? It started slowly and within a minute or two it was hard core. I couldn't keep up with the pace, I had sweat stains down to my waist and my muscles were screaming surrender, and that was after only ten minutes. It didn't look like I would make it to the first half hour. Eventually I figured out how to pace myself and got through the entire one-hour workout. Pacing myself came as a result of not being able to follow along all that well and so I had to stop and start again. Still even with the pacing, I was gasping for breath, but much to my surprise I felt pretty good after I caught my breath at the end of the class.

I didn't have any dinner, and having my fair share of groceries every day is critical to my survival, so we all went to our favorite restaurant for dinner. Normally I would order a burger, fries and a diet coke, but I decided on a salad and iced tea instead. I couldn't believe my own order – it was like someone had taken over my brain and ordered for me. What the heck was happening to me? Was I going to the fit and healthy dark side? I actually felt good about my choice. I was also pretty sure the new me wouldn't be around for long. I'm a realist okay.

I got home and after a quick shower I hit the sack without a bushel of food lying in my stomach or wheelbarrow of cookies on my night table to lull me into a carb induced snore fest. The next morning I did some stretching exercises, another first for me, then went to the kitchen and limited my breakfast intake to a bowl of Cornflakes with fruit and a cup of coffee. Mom thought I was coming down with something and checked my forehead for a fever. To complete my morning fitness program I got off the subway two stops early and walked the rest of the way to work. Seriously?

I put the picnic lunch that Natasha and me were going to share, in the fridge and went to my desk. Natasha came out of her office and said Georgette would arrive at nine thirty so she would return around ten o'clock. She gave me a conspiratorial wink and left the office.

At about ten after nine Georgette arrived. She was dressed in skinny jeans, an embellished t-shirt, sandals and an enormous bag. She had almost no make-up on and her skin had a healthy glow about it. Overall how she looked made me instantly hate her guts! Her hair swung when she walked for crap sake! My hair shifts when I walk.

"Hi, you must be Georgette, I'm Siobhan. Natasha called to say she would be a little late so why don't I get you a coffee, I haven't had one yet, and we can drink it in her office." "I'm a little early anyway. If you have stuff to do I'll go for a walk or something," she said. "No worries, I'm all caught up and waiting for Natasha to return to give me more work. Plus, I could use a cup of coffee before I walk her dogs. You have to be on your toes when you're walking that pair of horses," I said. Georgette started to laugh and went into Natasha's office. I put the cups and coffee pot on a tray and brought it in. I couldn't believe myself, totally slick talk. Major wow.

"You're new here right? How do you like working for Natasha?" she asked. "This is a summer job for me, but I hope to work part-time here when I go back to school. I really like working with Natasha, she's very kind and generous," I said. Georgette sat quietly for several seconds then she said. "You do know what this place is don't you?" "I know it's an escort service, which isn't illegal, but my job is mostly to do with Natasha's charities. How do you like working for Natasha?" I asked. "Me, I love my job. I get to wear fabulous clothes, make lots of money and hopefully meet a dishy, rich guy one day who will take care of me." I was stunned by what she said. I was staring at her trying to figure out if she was yanking my chain. She wasn't ages older than me, I think she was like twenty two or something, but she came off so shallow I was shocked. "You look surprised. I know that my ambitions aren't yours, but let's face it, I'm not a genius and my looks aren't going to last forever. I have to make hay while I can." "Oh I wasn't judging you, I was just a bit surprised that you didn't have bigger ambitions," I said. "Oh, trust me I've got big ambitions, but they don't involve me working too hard or breaking a sweat. I would like to open a dress shop one day. One that sells really high end, cute dresses. I would only sell the clothes to women if I like them and they looked cute in the dresses. You know what I mean? I wouldn't want ugly fat girls wearing my clothes," She said that, and looked straight at me. Could this pinhead, dummy be taking the piss out of me? If she was I would be very tempted to clock her, ignorant 'beatch'.

We sat chatting, for want of a better word, for the next ten minutes or so and then Natasha returned. Not a moment too soon I have to tell you. Long pointless stories are not my forte, although I have to say I was holding my own in that department. I got up and took the coffee service away and said goodbye to Georgette. "Let's get together sometime and have drink or something. We could get manicures and then have a girl's lunch. What do you say?" she asked. "That would be great. Call me when you have time and we can get together," I said and left the room.

About a half hour later Georgette left the office after waving goodbye. Shortly after Natasha called me into her office to hear what we had talked about. If I was a friend of Georgette's or even if I liked her, I would feel awkward being a tattle-tale, but I didn't have even the smallest amount of guilt when it came to Georgette. She was a major pill and a nitwit. I came to that conclusion after the first two minutes talking to her.

"So how did it go? Was she open with you?" Natasha asked. "Well first of all she's a bit of a bubble head. Her hobby is shopping and beauty treatments, not riding and whatever else is listed on her resume." "Oh that's just for show. It wouldn't be a good idea to list her hobbies as self-indulgent undertakings, now would it?" Natasha said. "I suppose you're right. Anyway she made it very clear that she loved her job because she made lots of money and wore beautiful clothes, but the biggest reason for her love of job was she got to meet 'dishy rich guys, who could take care of her', direct quote I might add. I asked her what her ambitions were and she said besides marrying one of these 'dishy rich guys', she thought she would like to open a dress store and sell cute dresses to cute girls. She made it very clear that she wouldn't sell her dresses to fat, ugly people, and she looked at me when she said that." After I finished relating my account of my meeting with Georgette, Natasha started to laugh. "Don't be offended by anything that little dimwit says. She is probably quite jealous of you. I'm interested though in the 'whole rich guys to take her away from it' all scenario. The men she has as clients consider her arm candy and nothing more, also most of them are either married, or in a relationship. Most of her clients are from out of town and prefer to have the same girl as an escort when they come to town on business. I'm concerned that there is more going on than escorting, and that isn't a good thing at all. Thank you Siobhan. I'll have to talk to Lucius and see what we need to do next." As I got up to leave I said, "How do girls like Georgette develop such an attitude? She seems unable to grasp the whole idea of her future and ambition."

"Girls like Georgette have been told their whole lives that they're beautiful, and they will always survive, and that there will always be someone to take care of them. It's a shame really because Georgette will never find what she's looking for. The whole attitude is quite Victorian."

I went out to the lobby to get Coco and Lola ready for their gallop. Either walking them was getting easier or I was getting stronger, whatever it was I was glad of the change.

After my minimal breakfast and extra physical activities I was pretty hungry by lunchtime. At about twelve-thirty I retrieved my skid load of lunch from the fridge, made some tea, and arranged everything in the dining room and went to get Natasha. "Oh boy I've been waiting all day for this." Over the next half hour we ate and talked, and ate some more. "My gosh your Mom is a heck of a cook. These sandwiches are divine and the cookies are heavenly." "My Mom will be thrilled that you like them. She loves to cook, and is happy when she has someone who appreciates her efforts. I try not to encourage her only because if she knew how much I loved her cooking, she would make twice as much of it, and I would be five times the size that I am now." Natasha was laughing as we packed up the leftovers. "Is it all right if I have the leftovers for dinner tonight? I'm not going out and it would be great not to have to worry about dinner. I think Lucius will love the veal." I looked at her and she smiled, "Don't worry we're good friends now, and enjoy many dinners together."

After work I walked three subway stops and then got on the train the rest of the way home. I was feeling tired but good. This whole fitness thing isn't so bad once you get started.

Dinner was a real family affair because my nutty Gran was visiting. After explaining to her about my job as well as school, friends and my life in general, I was able to slip out over to Marcy's. If I didn't get out of the house as quickly as possible I would have to repeat the entire conversation every hour on the hour for the rest of the night. I love my Gran to bits but her memory has a few leaks in it and that's putting it mildly.

When I got to Marcy's place she was waiting for me, and dying to know what went on with my Georgette meeting. I told her about Georgette, careful not leave any detail of her appearance or conversation out. When I told Marcy about the whole cute dresses for cute people thing she was furious. Marcy is very protective of my feelings and me. "She sounds like a total frigging drip to me.

Looking for a dishy rich guy to look after her. Can you imagine? How did you keep from cutting her a new one," she asked. "I know, it wasn't easy believe me. Maybe she wasn't referring to me when she said what she said, but I suspect that was her way of letting me know she was really superior to me." "So do you think she was into extras with her clients? It sure sounds that way." "I'm not sure maybe that talk was just for my benefit. I can tell you it would be bad news for her if she were adding extra services to her job, if you get my drift. I know Natasha would fire her ass in a heartbeat. I wonder which client she has in mind to take her away from it all. Or if she's found 'Mr. Rich, I'll take care of you' yet?"

I told Marcy about Rhode Island Commemorative Charity and she said she would do some searching herself. She had a summer job at the local library, and she knew how to find out information much better than me

Chapter 5

The rest of the week went by pretty quickly. Natasha decided on the photos I had suggested as a gift for the supporters of her latest charity event. On Friday Natasha told me that Gina would be in on Monday at nine thirty and we would do the same thing I had done with Georgette; meet her and draw her into a conversation about what she was doing and try and find out what was going on if anything.

I was happy to have the weekend to think about what was going on. Before I left on Friday Georgette called and asked if I would like to do something that night. I told her I was busy but we could maybe grab a coffee on Saturday or something. I gave her my cell number and I hung up. I wasn't busy but I figured a coffee with her was a lot better that going 'clubbing' which is what she suggested. The last thing I wanted to do was spend an evening with a fluffhead. That was way beyond anything in my job description.

I got home on Friday night and spent the evening with my parents and my grandmother. She was leaving the next day and she wanted to have an evening doing what she called 'girl stuff' with me and my Mom. I live such an exciting life.

My grandmother's idea of girl stuff was her talking about when she was a girl while she slurps back copious gin and tonics. The three of us sat in the kitchen eating junk food while Gran talked about her life as a teenager and young woman and the kind of underwear she used to wear and what the underwear did for her boobs and butt; way too much information for me. Of course she repeated herself constantly, and then she gave us a way too vivid description of her first sexual encounter, and then repeated the description at least five friggin' times during our 'girl's night'. No that is what I call a massive YIKES!!

Saturday morning about ten o'clock my phone rang and it's Georgette. I was hoping she would forget, but after hemming and hawing for five minutes about what I had to do that day we agreed to meet at a café at three o'clock.

At three I was waiting in the outdoor café for Georgette. I had dressed in jeans and one of my better casual tops. By three thirty she still hadn't showed up. I decided to give her another ten minutes then I was leaving. I hate sitting in a restaurant by myself sipping a drink, pretending like I really want to be there. I'm not much of a poser, as a matter of fact, I don't do the whole poser pretend thing at all.

Just as I'm gathering my handbag and getting up to leave she shows up. No apologies, no excuses, just the 'Oh hi' routine like we weren't supposed to be meeting at all, and she just happened to run into me. She plops down and immediately starts to rummage through her zillion dollar handbag for her cell phone. "I thought you said you wanted to meet at three o'clock?" "Did I? Well I'm never on time, and besides whoever is?" At that point I want to launch into a lecture reminding her that her time is not more valuable than mine, but decided against it. Instead I said, "I'm always on time. I don't like being late; it upsets me." If you thought that had an impact on her you would be totally wrong. "Whatever", was all she said.

She ordered some sort of low fat or fat free double cap half decaf confection I had no clue about, and proceeded to pick up her phone and make a call. I am doing a slow burn; I can't believe that anyone is so ignorant. Our drinks arrived and she finished her phone call. "So Siobhan, what kind of name is that anyway? Is it foreign name? Anyway it doesn't matter, how do you like working with Natasha and the sourpuss Lucius?" Before I got a chance to answer any of her questions she picked up her phone and started texting someone. I am ready to get up and leave. She didn't want to hang out, she just wanted someone in the seat opposite her in the café, so she wouldn't look like a damn loser. She was waving at people, picking up her phone every two seconds and basically acting like a total ass. Finally I'd had enough. I had wasted half my afternoon waiting for and then sitting with a complete dunderhead.

I finished my drink grabbed my bag and took out some money and put it on the table. "It's been swell, but I have to get going I'm meeting my friends for dinner." I stood up and she stopped what she was doing and said, "Can you wait until I finish my coffee? Maybe I could come with you and hang out some more. I don't have anything going on tonight. Natasha hasn't booked me, and I don't want to be by myself." I suddenly felt sorry for her. She really was a dummy, but she was a sad lonely dummy.

"Okay but we can't hang out tonight because it's a girlfriend night with just my close friends. Sorry." She looked disappointed but I thought there is no way I'm hanging out with her for an entire night. Besides, I didn't have anything planned with my friends. I lied, not nice, but there you go, I lied, so sue me. "In answer to your first question I quite like working for Natasha, and Lucius has been very nice to me. He's a bit quiet but I like him." "Oh, I thought maybe you took the job because you needed one. Natasha is really being bitchy lately. She doesn't seem to keen on booking me with my regulars anymore. She told me that they had asked for a change. I find that hard to believe I mean look at me. Why would any guy ask for a replacement?" My mouth must have been hanging open because she started to laugh. "Anyway if things don't improve, I'm moving on, I was thinking maybe I would start my own escort service. What do you think?"

I was shocked that she would ask me something like that, first of all her boss is also my boss, so how does she know I won't tell Natasha what she said? Secondly I don't know her from Adam and she doesn't know shit about me. I didn't answer her, and my silence must have sent her the message that I thought it was a great idea. Only a pea brain would come to that conclusion, but there you have it I was sitting opposite a major proportion pea brain. "I know it's a cool idea, a young with it woman running an escort service. I'm going to talk to some of the other girls who work for Natasha, and see what they say. Hey I have a great idea. Why don't you come work for me when I start up? Maybe you can even be an escort. Some guys might even like you, and you could make lots of money, if you know what I mean." I couldn't answer her, I had no words that would even come close to telling the bimbo how I really felt, so I just said, "I really have to go. Let's talk next week." I stood up to leave just as she picked up her phone. I waved goodbye and she nodded smiled and continued with her conversation.

My feelings of pity had quickly disappeared and were replaced with anger. Was she really that dim? The 'some guys might even like you' remark was making me major pissed off. Who the hell did she think she was? I stomped home I swear my feet barely touched the ground. When I got home I was a little less pissed and decided to call Marcy and see if she wanted to get together. The two of us met downtown so I could fill her in on all the shit the dimwith had said.

I told Marcy the whole story and she was totally shocked. "You cannot be serious. The whole story would be laughable if it wasn't so pathetic. Are you going to tell your boss?" "You bet, Natasha is my boss, and she's been really good to me. She trusts me, and I know she will want to know what Georgette is all about. I think she has a good idea but still, I plan on filling her in on all the details." "Georgette is going to find out you outed her. She's going to be pissed." "Like I give a rat's ass. She's the one who's all about the cute dresses for cute girls remember. I think she's a disgrace to women and a gigantic joke. Trouble is something in the back of my mind tells me she's also dangerous. I think a lot of her act is just that, an act."

Marcy and me talked for a while longer then went to the movies. We both live such incredibly exciting lives!

Chapter 6

I arrived at work little early and made the coffee. I had decided that I would bring Natasha a coffee and the two of us can have a chat about Georgette.

Natasha arrived at just after nine and after she settled in I brought her a coffee. "Can I have a word with you?' I asked. "Oh my you sound serious. I hope you aren't going to leave me or anything like that." I sat down in a chair facing her desk. "No nothing like that. It's concerning Georgette. I met her for coffee on Saturday."

I told Natasha the entire story from the fact that Georgette begged me to meet her, and then treated me like I was invisible, to her announcement that she was thinking of opening her own agency, and taking some of the girls with her. Usually I'm prone to adding a touch of exaggeration to a story, more of an embellishment actually. I believe a good story can only get better with some creative additions. This time I didn't lay it on. I didn't have to, it was a major story all by itself. Natasha said, "Well isn't that interesting. She's going to start her own agency and steal my girls and clients. I say good luck Georgette." "Oh yeah, I almost forgot this part, she asked me to come work for her. She also said I could be an escort if I wanted. Her words were 'Some guys might like you'," I said with a flourish that would be the envy of any

Broadway performer. Natasha sat with her mouth opened at the final remark. “Are you serious? She is that ignorant and insulting that she actually said that. I knew she was a self-possessed little bitch, but that remark goes way beyond ‘bitch’. I’m sorry that I put you in a situation where you were insulted by someone like her.” “No worries, I have a very healthy attitude about myself. No one like her could hurt my feelings. That’s a fact.” What I really wanted to do was kick her ass blue but of course I never told Natasha that. I didn’t want her to think I had a violent streak. I don’t actually, but kicking her ass was a tempting thought and if I were planning on becoming a violent type, her ass would be the recipient of my first bit of hostility.

We continued to talk for a while then it was time to walk the dogs. “Let’s talk again later today. I want to discuss this with Lucius.” I left Natasha staring out her window. She looked upset or angry, I’m not sure which. She definitely wasn’t happy. I don’t think she thought Georgette was going to ruin her business but I think she actually felt a tiny bit betrayed.

After returning from my doggie drag through the park, I went through my ‘to do’ list. One of the things I had to do was collect ‘silent auction’ items for the next big event, which was two months away. It was pretty easy to get some fairly impressive items for the auction. All I had to do was mention Natasha’s name and presto, no problemo.

Later in the day Lucius arrived, “Is she in her office?” he asked. I nodded and he went right in. The two of them spent the next couple of hours behind the closed door of Natasha’s office. About three o’clock Lucius popped his head out, “Siobhan can you join us for a chat.” Uh oh, I thought I’m going to get the boot. I should never have told her everything. I should never have had coffee with that dimwit Georgette. Drats, I am such an a-hole. I stood up from my desk and followed Lucius into Natasha’s office, I felt like I was walking the plank.

"Sit down Siobhan. Lucius and I would like to talk to you about what you told me this morning regarding Georgette." I knew it! I should have kept the whole thing to myself, now I was having to face the dour Lucius. "Yes, I'm sorry I told you. I thought you should know, but maybe I should have kept it to myself, maybe I shouldn't have met her for coffee, but you did tell me to get close. Please don't fire me I really like my job," I said completely blowing my cool. "My goodness we wouldn't dream of firing you, we wondered if you could help us with Georgette." I stood staring at the two of them and then kind of snapped out of it when I heard they weren't going to can me. "Sit down, let's have a chat. Lucius and I have an idea how we can deal with our little friend Georgette, but we need your help." I was so relieved I felt giddy. This was going to be interesting.

"We'd like you to get closer to Georgette. Encourage her, and try to get her to take you into her confidence. She isn't a terribly bright girl, and we're pretty sure she didn't come up with the idea of opening her own escort service all by herself. We think that she has someone backing her, but we don't know who that someone is. You could get her talking about her plans, and hint that might join her once she's up and running. What do you think? We just want to know who her partner is. We really don't care terribly about Georgette." Natasha said. I thought about it for a minute or two and then said, "I'll do whatever you want me to do no problem. Do you really think she'll confide in me? She doesn't know me at all." "Well we think, because she told you what she had in mind after just a few minutes during your coffee get together, that she'll spill the beans because she likes you, and also she doesn't understand the basics of discretion," Lucius said. "I agree with you there. She is totally indiscreet, like crazy indiscreet actually. Do you really think she likes me? If she does she sure has a strange way of showing it.

She basically spent most of the time we were together talking on the phone, and acting like a princess jerk. To be honest I thought she was horrible, bad mannered and very rude," I said. "I hate to say it, but that's what she's like. She's very good looking, but not to swift. She is convinced the world should pay homage to her because of her looks," Natasha said.

We sat talking for another ten minutes discussing what the next moves were and what I should say to Georgette. I was enjoying the whole cloak and dagger thing but I was feeling a little nervous about being an undercover agent for Natasha and Lucius.

I went back to my desk, and at the end of the day Natasha told me that Gina, the other questionable escort, would be in to see her in the morning. We agreed to do the same sort of thing we had done when Georgette had come in for a meeting. I was hoping that this Gina babe wasn't as big a bitch as Georgette. I can only take so much jerky attitude per week. One coffee meet with Georgette and I was close to my limit for the week, no make that the friggin' month.

When I got home I changed into sweats for my Zumba class. Mom insisted on packing me a snack to eat at the break. I didn't want to bother explaining that there is no break. If I did explain, it wouldn't matter anyway because she'd probably tell me that I can dance and eat at the same time. She is convinced that moving while eating puts you in the negative category when it comes to calories. Who am I to argue with that kind of logic?

Marcy and me went back to her place after the Zumba sweat fest and ate my Mom's snacks, and I told her about what Natasha and Lucius had asked me to do. "That could be dangerous. Suppose Georgette's silent partner is a mobster or something like that? You could get your legs broken or even worse." "What are you talking about? Mobsters, broken legs, danger, all I'm going to do is get the little pinhead to spill on her plans." "Well I don't care what you say, you should be careful. If you need help, let me know. Or if you want me to like sit at another table to be like a spotter type person when you meet her again, I can do that, then if she gives you trouble or something I'll be there." I had to laugh, the vision of Marcy sitting two tables away wearing a trench coat, a big hat and a pair of sunglasses, and reading a newspaper made me laugh. "Let me think about it. It might not be such a bad idea," I said. I told Marcy about my meeting with the other wayward escort, Gina. "Suppose they both have the same plans or this Gina person has a different set of problems, you could be up to you pits in wacky escorts," Marcy said. She was right. This was a summer job and nothing more. Now I was playing Nancy Drew and could find myself in all kinds of crap I didn't plan on being in. "You're right Marc, I'm going to follow through on the Georgette thing, because I said I would, and then I think I'll tell Natasha that my espionage days are over."

Chapter 7

I was more than a little nervous about meeting Gina. I was thinking, suppose she's the same as Georgette, and what if she wants to start her own agency as well? That would be totally too much for me, I'm too young for that kind of crap. If that happened I would definitely have to tell Natasha that I'm giving up my sleuthing career, and resigning my undercover job even if she fires me and I have to go back to serving burgers at some 'chew and choke'. It would be way too much for me if I this Gina babe were another 'would be' turncoat. I don't know why I was getting my knickers in such a knot, it was a summer job, not a lifelong career. I decided that if Gina tells me something that is not quite kosher, I'm going to keep it to myself. At least I thought I would.

Natasha had made the same arrangements with Gina as she had with Georgette and so I was in the office when Gina arrived to meet with Natasha. "Hi, you must be Gina. Natasha is going to be a little late. Why don't you go into her office and I'll bring us both a cup of coffee, I haven't had any yet this morning," I said. "No probs" Gina said and stomped into Natasha's office.

Gina was very good looking, in a tarty sort of way. She was about five foot six, slim and muscular. She had a lot of big hair, it actually looked kind of wiggish. Her skirt was tight and short, her shoes were like stilts, at least to me they were; I'm a wedge heel kind of gal. She had a pair of whacking big boobs that were encased in a bandeau type top and she wore a see through blouse over the bandeau. Overall the effect was quite cheap looking. It struck me that she was in a costume, and the whole look was overtly slutty, like she planned to look like a slut. I couldn't imagine why Natasha hadn't had a chat with Gina about her personal appearance. Perhaps the look she presented on her day off was different than her working outfit.

When I brought the coffee into Natasha's office Gina was standing by the window staring at the street below. She turned as I walked into the room, and she followed me to the sofa. "Perfect, I haven't had a cup yet today. What's your name?" "Siobhan Murphy" I answered. "Gina Prospero, nice to meet you. You're new here right? Do you like working here? Don't get me wrong it's an okay place to work, but you seem pretty ordinary. If you get my drift." I didn't get her drift. What was so ordinary about me? Was it the fact that I didn't normally wear 'big hair' except in the humidity, or was it because I wore sensible shoes and a skirt to my knees? "I'm not sure I know what you mean by that comment. What's wrong with working here? Natasha is really great to work for. The money is good, and the job is interesting. No downside at all to this place that I can see." I was getting a little defensive and I didn't know why. I felt like Gina was testing me. "Hey don't take offence, I meant none. I'm just makin' small talk is all." Great I had made a mountain out a friggin' molehill. "Sorry I thought you were being smartass, and I overreacted. Actually I feel lucky to get this job. It's just for the summer, but it's fun and the money is better than most places. How do you like working for Natasha?" I asked hoping my apology and explanation would suffice. "I like it fine. It's not my life's work but it pays the bills, and right now that's the name of the game." After the initial sort of combativeness, mine not hers, had disappeared from our conversation we actually had a pretty good time talking. “Let’s get together for a drink this week sometime.” Gina said. “Sure what about Thursday?” Gina checked her schedule on her Blackberry and said “Perfect, I’ll call you Thursday morning and we can decide where to meet.” At that moment Natasha walked in and I left the room and went back to my desk. I had a couple of problems with the whole drink scenario. First of all I’m underage and second, I can’t imagine where Gina would want to meet to have the drinks she’s talking about. Maybe I could talk her into coffee and dessert somewhere. Gina had to be in her mid-twenties. Why would she want to hang out with a kid like me? Especially have a drink with me. I don’t get that at all. Georgette was different naïve and totally stupid, but Gina was smart and she certainly didn’t need a kid like me to hang with. Maybe it was my magnetic personality and incredible charm that convinced her that I would be someone she should hang out with. Hey you never know.

After returning from walking the beasts Natasha came out to see me. “So what did you think of Gina?” “ I like her,” I said. “She’s a little rough around the edges, but she’s nice, once you get past the exterior.” Natasha smiled and said she agreed with me. She said she couldn’t see Gina breaking the rules, and she certainly couldn’t imagine her doing what Georgette was planning. When she said that I remembered, although I hadn’t actually forgotten, that I had to meet ‘Miss Obnoxious’ at some point this week. I felt quite sick about it, if you want to know the truth. The whole undercover, secret agent thing wasn’t doing it for me. It made me nervous and when I’m nervous I tend to sweat like a pig.

“I’m going to set something up with Georgette this week like you suggested. What should I ask her? Do you want to know who she’s taking with her or who her silent partner is?” I asked. “I would like to know what she has in mind in terms of my clients and staff. I'd also like to know who is behind this. It isn't her big idea, that's for sure. She just isn't that smart," Natasha said. "Hmm, I have figure out how I'm going to do that without looking nosy. Got any ideas?" I asked. Natasha smiled and said, "I think you're pretty good on your feet, you'll figure something out. If all else fails tell her you're nosy and then get up and leave. She's got a hide like a rhino. I don't think you can insult her or hurt her feelings. Don't worry about it. Find out what you can, that's all I ask. The minute you feel uncomfortable with any of this, just tell me."

After I spoke to Natasha she left my office and Georgette called wanting to get together. We set up a something for the next day. I wasn't looking forward to it at all.

I decided to walk all the way home, I wanted to formulate a plan for my Georgette encounter, and I also needed to walk off the gigantic lunch I had consumed. I swear I'm an eating machine, my stomach never bothers sending a signal to my brain letting it know that it's has enough fuel to last a week. Needless to say once I stop chowing down my waistband is tight and my trousers feel like I'm wearing a pair of Spanx, and I wish I were in my comfy track pants.

When I got home Mom was waiting for me, "Some girl named Georgette just called here looking for you. She wants you to give her a call as soon as you get in. Did you turn off your cell? She said she tried to call you on your cell phone but couldn't reach you. You're a bit late did you have to work late tonight?" I told my Mom about walking home, "I had my cell turned off. I wanted to think." I decided to tell my Mom about what was going on at work and what I was supposed to find out for Natasha. "Gosh honey, I don't like the sounds of that. It's kind of sneaky, and not really part of your job. Do you really want to do that?" "Natasha has been really good to me and I feel like I owe her my help. If it gets uncomfortable or awkward for me, I'm going to back off. I better phone Georgette and find out what she wants." I knew my Mom was going to tell my Dad what I was doing, and he wouldn't like it at all. Both my parents are pretty protective of me and my dad in particular would be all over anyone who tried to hurt me in any way.

Chapter 8

I went to my room, sat on the bed, and called Georgette. She answered right away, and asked if we could get together tomorrow after work. I told her that I was around, and we agreed to meet at the same place we had gone before.

The next day, when I got to work, I went into Natasha's office to tell her about my date with Georgette after work. "I'm kind of nervous. Suppose she asks me to work for her, what should I say to her?" "Tell her you'll let her know. Say that you have to talk it over with your parents. Try and get as much information as you can about her new company. Make no commitment just listen, and tell her you'll get back to her. I'd like to find out where the money is coming from for her new venture. Besides the fact that she's a bit of a brainless twit, she's definitely not the type of person who would have saved her pennies to start her own business."

After working all day I went in to say goodbye to Natasha. "Good luck dear, call me tonight and let me know how things went."

I took the subway all the way home to save time. I wanted to have some dinner and change before meeting Miss Pinhead. I got home and had my dinner. After dinner I went to my room to change, and kind of sort my head out. I didn't tell my folks where I was going but did say I wouldn't be long. I definitely didn't want to tell my Mom I was meeting Georgette. She and dad would have probably followed me.

I arrived at the café and of course Georgette wasn't there waiting. Did I think she would be? Nope. Ignorance is bliss. After ordering an ordinary coffee, apparently not done in this particular café, because the 'head up his bum' waiter said the word 'regular coffee' like his mouth was full of dog shit, I sat and flipped through a magazine I had brought while waiting for her highness to make her appearance.

Finally, twenty minutes late, Georgette showed up and once again no apologies were given. She sat down, pulled out her phone and put some papers on the table. I was fully expecting her to pick up her phone and start texting one of her loser friends, but she didn't. "How are you Siobhan, it's good to see you." Whoa, who is this person? She was actually polite and almost human. "Good to see you. What's going on with you?" I said matching her polite human-like tone. "Cool, let's get down to business. Oh, just a bit of advice, you shouldn't wear that color, it makes you look like a turnip." Did you ever feel like one of those cartoon characters who 'blows his stack' in temper and has smoke blowing out of his ears? That's what I felt like. "That does it, you are a bad mannered, ignorant trout. I am out of here." I was livid, which is a something that rarely happens to me. I couldn't believe the bitch, I didn't need her crap and to hell with Natasha and her sleuthing. "Siobhan, please don't go. I didn't mean what I said. I just shoot off my mouth all the time, and never think before I speak. I'm stupid. Please stay," she said and then started to cry. Now let me say something about crying. There are good-looking criers and ugly ones. Georgette was some ugly; yes, there is a god and there is justice. She was grotesque, sitting there with a scrunched up face and makeup down to her ass. "What did you expect me to do? Sit and take you criticism and barbs like I'm some sort of dummy. I'll stay but try and keep your comments civil or you can drink your coffee by yourself." I sat down and after she mopped up her face and pulled herself together we talked.

"Before I made that ignorant cow remark, I wanted to show you my business plan for my new escort service." She pushed an envelope toward me and I opened it up and took out a fairly professional looking document. I browsed through it without really focusing on anything in particular. What do I know about business plans anyway? Zippety-do-da that's what! The only thing I'm really looking for is a hint of who the person is behind this big shot plan. "Who are your partners?" I asked. "I can't tell you that without a commitment from you. Sorry, but they made me promise not to blab." She said the word 'they' so that means she probably has two or three other people involved. I'm pretty sure she's the face of the agency and that's it for her 'business' involvement.

"First of all, I'm a student and will be going back to school in the fall, so my time commitment would be very part time. Secondly, what kind of job do you want me to do for you? Surely you could hire anyone for the job. Why me?" Georgette sat staring at me for a couple of seconds. She kind of threw a blank I think. Anyway, she sort of shook her head and answered, "I want you to work for me because I trust you. I know you're smart, and you would have my back. You could work any hours you want, and I'd be happy." I sat thinking for a few minutes then I said, "Let me think about it. I'll let you know in the next few days. I want to talk to my folks about it. Is that okay with you?" She nodded, "Yes talk to your parents about it, and then let me know."

After about fifteen more minutes of airhead talk from Georgette we both got up to leave. She hugged me and apologized again for being such a major jackass, and for a nano second I felt a tad guilty about my subterfuge, but like I said for a nano second, and then I was over it.

Chapter 9

I had a lot to think about so I called my bestie Marcy to talk about it. I was feeling caught in the middle of something that was way outside of my comfort zone, seriously way far out of my comfort zone. I told Marcy the whole deal with Georgette including the 'turnip' comment. Marcy freaked, "The ignorant bitch calling you a turnip. I would have ploughed her," she said. I told her how I'd gotten up to leave and she had started the old tears routine, and been so apologetic and pathetic that I gave a second chance. Of course, I also told Marcy about how gross looking Georgette became when she cried. "I love it! Life is fair after all. But really I think I would have kept on walking. You're way to nice sometimes."

"I would have felt guilty if I had kept on walking. I have to say I'm not sure I want to continue with this whole undercover thing. I feel nervous and creepy about it. It is so not me. What do you think?" I asked. "If it was me I'd follow through, but cover you ass by keeping me in the loop and all that sort of thing. Write down everything that has happened, you know, like keep a diary of events. Also don't think of it as undercover, think of it as detecting, like detective work," Marcy said. "I don't know about detective work but you're right. Tomorrow I'm going to report to Natasha everything that Georgette told me and see what she says. I also have to meet Gina this week. At least she's a little more real than fluffhead Georgette. I'll let you know what the scoop is tomorrow night." After I hung up from Marcy I gave Natasha a call. I told her I'd fill her in on my evening with Georgette the next day.

I didn't sleep very well that night; I couldn't get Georgette out of my mind. I felt nervous for her, like she was in danger or something, and don't ask me why I felt like that, I just did. Maybe it was just all the day's activities rolled together that made me feel unsettled. My alarm went off just as I drifted into a deep sleep. Just what I needed an entire day of dead head.

I got up and dressed and was having a coffee in the kitchen when my phone rang. It was Natasha. She told me Lucius was going to pick me up and to sit tight, he could be a few minutes late. I was pretty happy for the ride to work let me tell you. I was so tired my legs felt like lead, and I could easily have slept on a pin. I took my time with breakfast, scarfing back a whole whack of toast and peanut butter; I get hungry when I'm tired. After taking my time with my cup of joe and toast the doorbell rang and I answered it to Lucius.

"Hi Lucius, I'll be right with you." I said as I grabbed my stuff, said goodbye to my Mom and headed towards the door. Outside I asked him "How come you're picking me up today? Are we going to Saks or to breakfast?" I hoped it was Saks, even I couldn't handle another breakfast. "We're meeting Natasha at Saks and then we're going to her condo." I was under the impression that she lived where she worked. Upstairs or something so I asked him "You mean she doesn't live at the brownstone?" "She has a suite there but she lives uptown in a condo. Very few people know about her home, she likes to keep it private," he said.

We arrived at Saks and joined Natasha as she picked out a few cocktail dresses for the girls. There was another reception coming up and she wanted to add a few new outfits to the collection. She had, once again, picked out an outfit for me and just as I was about to object she said, "Siobhan, I know you are going to argue with me about buying you another outfit, I need you to look good for the reception, as well as an event for one of my charities that is coming up. Like I said before, consider it a uniform." Who could argue with that kind of logic? Not this kid!

After we finished shopping we drove to Natasha's condo. We pulled up to a canopied entrance, complete with a doorman wearing a fancy ass uniform, very swish. We got out of the car and Mr. Swishy uniform held the door for us and we stepped into the lobby, which was awesome with marble floors, wood paneled walls, expensive furniture, palm trees and sparkly chandeliers. It wasn't ultra-modern it was kind of old fashioned rich, I made that up I don't know what old fashioned rich looks like, how would I? It was a feeling like old money and castles in Europe. We got on the elevator and went to the penthouse. The elevator opened right into Natasha's suite, again, awesome, and I walked into this black and white marble foyer lit with crystal chandeliers. I whistled underneath my breath. "Totally beautiful, it's like a movie set," I said. "Thank you Siobhan, I love every room in my apartment. I decorated the condo just for me, I'm very lucky I could do that," Natasha said. She showed me around her place and of course every room was a total gem. I was taking mental pictures so I could tell my Mom and Dad about the place when I got home that night.

"Come into the living room Siobhan, we'll have a coffee and you can tell me all about your evening with Georgette." We sat down in the living room, which by the way was totally unbelievable. I could seriously have lived in that room. I told her about the business plan and that Georgette had a couple of partners. "I'm pretty sure she is just a face and not the brains. She didn't appear to have a clue about the operation. I asked her why she wanted me to work there and she said she need someone she could trust." "Did she tell you who her backers were? Did she even give you a hint?" Natasha asked. "I asked her directly who her partners were and she told me that she couldn't say anything unless I agreed to work for her. At that stage I figured I had gotten everything I could out of her, and to be honest I had had enough of her company." Natasha and Lucius both laughed, "I understand completely dear, you are doing a huge favor for us and it is appreciated. Now we need to figure out what to do next, any ideas Lucius, Siobhan?

Lucius and I looked at each other than at Natasha, "I haven't got a clue what to do next. If I tell her I'm going to work for her then what? Do you think she's ready to go with her new business in the next few weeks?" I asked. "I seriously doubt it. They would have needed to line up a lot of girls, find a place to operate from, set up a marketing and sales program, the whole nine yards. No, I think they are in the early planning stages and Georgette is the only thing they have lined up for sure. I think we play it slow. You can get to know her better, if you can stomach it, and in the meantime Lucius and I will do a little background searching of our own."

The three of us sat talking about everything but Georgette for another half hour or so. "I'd better get to the office, Gina is going to call today and I don't want to miss her call," I said. "Gina, I forgot about Gina. When are you going to meet her? Or are you? You must be tired of spending your off hours snooping for us," Natasha said. "Actually Gina is okay. Well at least she seems okay, but you never know she might turn out to be a total jack ass." "Well if you don't mind meeting Gina, and spending time with her we really appreciate it. You can let us know after you meet her, what she said and your gut feeling about her."

Lucius and I left Natasha, who was going to work from home, and headed to the office. I got back to my desk in time to get a call from Gina. We decided to meet that night for a drink at a local bar. I'm to young to drink, and to be honest I don't like the taste of alcohol anyway, I generally go for a diet soda or fruit juice. I checked myself in the mirror, and figured I looked okay and wouldn't have to go home to change.

I had to take Lola and Coca for a walk, so after cleaning up the messages and organizing my desk I grabbed their leads and called for Mr. Personality with the shit scooper, to come for a walk with me and the horses. Once we hit the dog park part of the park, and I had released the hounds, so to speak, I went to find a place to sit down leaving the poop scooper to do his job. As I sat thinking about stuff, Georgette, Gina, Natasha, the whole freaking lot, I looked up and there, off under a tree, swapping spit like a couple of teenagers was Georgette and some guy. I stared for a minute or so and then skulked over to a tree opposite them and watched for a while longer. It was a real love fest, and it would have been all warm and fuzzy if it had been anyone else but Georgette. I wanted to yell 'get a room', instead I took out my phone and decided to capture the Kodak moment. I waited until Romeo came up for air, and gave me a full frontal before I took the pictures. I decided to show them to Natasha the next day and see if she recognized the dude.

Meanwhile, after twenty minutes of frolicking and pooping the dogs were ready to go home. I gathered up their leashes, snapped them on and they pulled me back to the office.

After depositing the dogs with Jenkins I went to my office. I wanted to upload the pictures I had taken, and forward them to Natasha. After I had the pictures up on the screen I thought I would take a closer look and see if I recognize Romeo from the reception. I enlarged the picture, and as I was looking at it I noticed someone off to one side of the two lovers. Hot damn this was like CSI for crap sake. I isolated that section of the picture and blew it up as big as I could and there armed with a camera was Gina! She was taking pictures of Georgette and her guy. What the hell was going on? Why would Gina take pictures of Georgette necking in the park? I sat back in my seat and stared at my computer trying to sort out what to do. Finally, after tossing things around in my tiny feeble mind, I decided not to show anything to Natasha. I decided that I wanted to find out what was going on myself. I certainly didn't want to stir the shit if there was no reason for stirring. Besides, I was having a good time playing Nancy Drew. I liked Gina, and I wanted to know what she was doing in the park, so I printed the picture to bring with me that night. I was going to wait and see how the evening with her progressed before I showed her the photo. That sounded like I knew what I was doing. NOT.

I decided to remove the pictures I had uploaded, and after thinking about stuff until my head hurt, I went to get ready. By getting ready I mean plastering down my out of control mop of hair with a pound of lard (styling gel) and a headband. I scrubbed my face and applied some cream and a bit of makeup. Who am I kidding? I overloaded on the makeup hoping to make myself look older and more sophisticated. Of course, I knew once I applied it, stood back from the mirror and did a quick assessment of the extra 'color' I had added I would be ready to wash it off. I was trying to remember how the guy who did my makeup for the reception did it. Anyway I finally sorted myself out and looked okay, not stunning but okay. I'm not a tire biter or anything like that, I just haven't got a clue how to put it all together.

I still had a bit of time before I was supposed to meet Gina so I gave Marcy a call. After a couple of minutes of ordinary gossip I filled her in on my espionage in the park.

"Holy, holy, holy, holy. What's all that about? What are you going to do about it?" I thought one less 'holy' would probably work a bit better, but when Marcy has a theme going she's like a dog with a bone. "I'm going to do a more little snooping on my own before I do anything. I want to find out what Gina was doing taking pictures," I said. "You be careful, these guys could mean big trouble. Maybe I should shadow you at the bar," Marcy said. 'Shadow' I wondered what the hell was she talking about. I wanted to tell her to stop watching cop shows but, I didn't want to hurt her feelings so I said, "Maybe that's not such a bad idea. You have to promise to be absolutely discreet though. Otherwise the whole thing could blow up in my face." Marcy agreed and I told her where I would be meeting Gina. "I'm going to head over the bar in about a half hour so I'd better let you go so you can get down there before me," I said, and then hung up.

After I took a quick final look in the bathroom mirror and left the office.

Chapter 10

I arrived at the bar and looked around trying to spot Marcy. At first I didn't see her but spotted Gina at a table in the corner. Just as I waved and walked toward Gina, I noticed Marcy sitting by herself at another table wearing a pair of big black framed glasses and way too much lipstick and hairspray. She looked at me, gave me a little nod and went back to her soda. I had to compose myself so I wouldn't start laughing, Marcy can be such an asswipe at times, and I mean that in the best and nicest possible way. I sat down at Gina's table and she said, "Hey, how are you? You look a little nervous, anything wrong?" Shit how transparent am I? I'm trying to be cool and this babe picks out my jumpiness right away. "No I'm fine, just a busy day that's all. How are you doing?" Gina smiled a sort of smirky type smile. Is that even a word? Anyway she looked quite cool and not at all like a person taking sneaky pictures. "I've been taking it easy. I'm trying to decide what courses I'm going to take in the fall." "Are you in school?" I asked. "You didn't think I'd be doing what I'm doing to make as my life's work did you?" I was kind of shocked and a tad confused. I thought she was hardcore and into the whole escort thing. "I just assumed you were in it for the long haul, maybe saving for your own business or something like that. That doesn't sound right. I'm sorry, I just don't know anything about you, and I made some guesses that were clearly not too accurate." I was totally out of my element and at a loss for words. I felt like a jerk.

After we got over my dumbass ignorance we talked about everything from favorite food to clothes and my majors at school. Everything was going fine, and then before I knew it she was asking me questions about my work and Natasha. She was really subtle about it, but she was questioning me. I began to feel a little awkward, and I didn't like it. I decided to confront her with the picture I had taken. Two can play at that game, I think. I dig into my trunk of a handbag, I bring to work everyday, and pulled out the envelope that I had the picture in. As Gina talked about Natasha and her 'gig' I handed her the picture. No preliminary for me, no sirree, just straight up confrontation. "What's this?" Gina asked. I then pulled out the second shot with her detail blown up. "That's you taking a picture of Georgette in the park today. What are you some kind of spy or something?" Gina sat staring at the pictures for quite a while before she said anything, "How did you get this? Did you take it? How many other people know about this? Did you show this to Natasha?" She looked a bit panicky and I felt like a total shit. "Take it easy, I took the picture when I was at the dog park today. I spotted Georgette with some guy and took a picture. When I got back to the office I uploaded it intending to see if Natasha knew the guy at all. As I was blowing it up I spotted you in the corner. Don't worry, no one knows about it. I wanted to ask you what was going on first before I tell Natasha. So what gives?" Gina sat for a minute or so before she answered, "Okay, here's the thing before I tell you anything you have to swear you won't tell anyone what I tell you." She was dead serious so I told her I would never tell anyone anything. I was kind of tired of being the person with all the secrets if you know what I mean. "I swear I won't mention a word, unless of course you're a terrorist, then I'm contacting Homeland Security, or the CIA or FBI or whatever." "Okay. Just a minute." She dug into her purse, which made me jump out of my skin, I figured she was going to pull out a gun. The fact that we were in a crowded restaurant had not occurred to me at that point. My eyes must have been like saucers and she said, "Take it easy it's not a gun it's my badge, I'm an undercover cop." She flashed something shiny past me and then returned it to her purse. I sat staring at Gina with my mouth hanging open. You could probably have driven an eighteen-wheeler into my mouth no problemo.

"You're an undercover cop? What are you doing at Natasha's? She doesn't do anything wrong, why are you investigating her?" Gina stared at me for a couple of seconds and then said, "I can't tell you that, but what I can tell you is we aren't necessarily watching Natasha. She's a pretty good old broad actually, and I think she's pretty above board." "Well then what are you doing there? Why take pictures of Georgette?" Gina thought for a couple of seconds before she answered, "I can't tell you right now okay. It would put you in danger as well as me. I just need you to promise not to tell anyone about me, or months of work will go down the drain. Will you promise?"

I was stunned and not sure what to say. Should I tell her that I was supposed to be checking her out for Natasha? Should I fill her in on what Georgette had told me about her new business plans? Or should I quit my job and go and work for a Chew and Choke and be done with it? I was really torn, on the one hand I loved my job and the money was good. On the other hand it could be dangerous and messed up, and I could wind up being caught in the middle of something that I didn't understand. Of course all these notions flew through my brain in a nano second. I knew without too much strain on my brain that I wasn't going to quit, I was having a blast and besides why should I let anyone intimidate me. No, I had the upper hand and I held all the cards, at least I thought I did. "Don't worry I won't tell anyone. But you'd better be careful, Natasha and Lucius aren't thick, they'll figure out what you're doing eventually. I know you can't tell me what you're looking for, but maybe I might hear something that would help you." What was I doing? I was asking her if she wanted help with her undercover operation. I was joining the dark site, I swear I had a temporary loss of sanity. YIKES!

"That's very generous. I appreciate that you won't drop me in it by spilling the beans. If you do hear anything it would be great if you let me know. Why don't we plan to meet here every week at the same time and day?" I nodded and said, "Okay, that would be good. I'm not going to snoop around for you or anything like that, but if I do hear or see stuff I think is weird I'll let you know." Gina smiled and looked pretty relieved. I don't know what she thought I would do anyway. I'm a good law-abiding citizen for crap sake. That sounds pretty scary actually.

The two of us sat for a few more minutes and talked about stuff other than Natasha's place. Gina was pretty nice actually. She said this undercover thing was going to give her career a big boost if it worked out. Eventually she got up to leave so I got up as well. I really wanted to talk to Marcy but I couldn't tell Gina the cop that I had staked the place out! Listen to me, way too many cop shows. I followed her out the door and gave Marcy the eye on the way out. I hoped she would figure out and recognize that the 'eye' meant, 'meet me at the Starbucks down the street in ten minutes'. After I said goodbye to Gina I walked towards the coffee shop. I ducked into a store doorway and looked back to make sure Gina was gone. I could see her walking off into the distance and then saw Marcy leave the bar and head my way. Amazing what a well-placed 'eyeball' look says to your best friend.

I went to the coffee shop, ordered giant latte, a brownie and two cookies, and sat down in the corner, and waited for Marcy. Five minutes later she arrived, still in disguise, she looked around, went to the counter ordered some sort of whipped cream concoction, and then after another quick sweep of the café again, she sat down in front of me.

I appreciated what Marcy was doing to help me, but I have to tell you it took everything I had not too wet my pants laughing.

"How'd it go? Never mind, look over my shoulder to see if I was followed." I looked over her shoulder like she asked and then said, "Relax you weren't followed 007, and take off the disguise, you're going to make me laugh." I had been trying to decide whether to tell Marcy about Gina being an undercover cop. Marcy wasn't a big mouth or anything like that, I just didn't want to get her involved. It could be a pretty messy situation. Then I thought she's already involved so what's the difference. So I told her. I think she said the word 'holy' about one hundred and fifty times followed by 'shit', 'shit' and 'double shit'.

Chapter 11

I got home that night and my parents were up watching TV, "Siobhan, where've you been? Your boss called and your friend Georgette called, you're pretty popular today. Come on in and have a snack and tell us about your day." Keeping my mouth shut when it comes to my parents is a challenge. My folks are the best and I always feel compelled to tell them everything that's going on in my life, if I don't I always feel guilty. This time I knew I had to edit my day big time or my dad would be all over it. He's a big law and order guy everything above board and honest. The three of us went into the kitchen and in between inhaling one of my mom's lemon meringue pies I told them about my day. Not all the details, but a strictly edited version. My mom's lemon meringue pie is a thing of beauty. A crispy buttery crust, tangy, sweet, sunny yellow lemon filling topped with a mile high layer of meringue – yum. Every time my mom plunks a piece of it down in front of me I feel like saluting.

After consuming my weight in pie I went up to my room. I decided to take a shower and then make an early, sort of, night of it. I also needed to figure out what I was going to say to Natasha, Georgette, Gina, and all the rest of the cast of characters who had invaded my normal, boring life.

The next morning I walked most of the way to work. I was still trying to work out what I was going to tell Natasha. I also knew that I needed to have a conversation with Georgette at some point today.

When I got to the office and sat down at my desk Natasha came out, "I got your message that you called but it was kind of late. Sorry I didn't call back." I said. "That's okay dear. I was just curious to find out how your thing with Gina went. Why don't we sit down in an hour or so and have a chat." I had one hour to sort out my story. While I was sitting there giving my brain a workout Georgette called, "Didn't you get my message last night?" "Yes I did, I didn't get home until late so I decided not to call. I was just going to get in touch with you this morning," I said. "Where were you last night? Were you out with a guy or something? I can't imagine. Sorry I don't mean it like that, I just can't picture you on a date," she said. What a jackass, "You're a total jerk you know that. You don't know anything about me. Who the hell do you think you are?" I then slammed the phone down not once but several times. Must be my Irish temper. Of course the dimwit called back and I continued to hang up. "Hello, piss off" click, "Hello, bite me" click, you get the idea. Of course, I fully expected her to turn up at the office. Someone like Georgette may be a total ignoramus, but she needs people to like her. I knew she didn't mean what she said. Actually she did mean it, she just hasn't figured out how to stop whatever dumbass piece of shit remark that pops into her empty head, from coming out of her lip-lined and glossed stupid mouth unedited.

I had decided what to tell Natasha. I was going to show her a cropped picture of Georgette and her guy – I definitely didn't want her to see Gina. I was going to tell her that Gina was a good egg, and she needn't worry about her loyalties.

I knocked on Natasha's door and then went in, "Come in, sit down. I heard you slamming the phone down a minute ago. Is everything okay?" I told her about Georgette and she started to laugh, "Sorry, I'm not laughing at you; it's Georgette, she has no idea how to behave. Her manners and conduct are deplorable. It will be interesting to see how she survives as she gets older and her looks start to go by way of the dodo bird." "You mean her boobs down to her waist, and she got some sort of turkey jowl, gobbler type action going on under her chin?" I said. Natasha started to laugh and after a few seconds I joined in the laughter and the two of us were howling a minute later.

After we both caught our breath and wiped the tears from our eyes I told her about my evening with Gina, "I like her. She's pretty straight, no phoniness at all about her. I don't know what her future plans are but she seems pretty above board to me." "I figured as much. It was just a niggling feeling I had about Gina. I think it's just her rather brusque attitude." Without too much drama – I'm trying to tone it down – I produced the photo of Georgette. "I was in the park walking the dogs when I spotted Georgette, here you take a look," and I handed the pictures to Natasha. "What's this?" "Take a look at them. I blew up the face of the guy she was with. I didn't recognize him from your last reception, but I thought maybe you would." Natasha took two seconds to identify the guy. "Oh, I know who he is. I know exactly who and what he is. This guy is her financier, no question about it. He came to a couple of my receptions but he wasn't our kind of client and so he wasn't invited again. When I stopped inviting him to our receptions Georgette was all over it, wanting to know why he wasn't invited and all that stuff. He is a pretty dangerous guy. He told us he was a financial analyst, but I'm pretty sure his business has nothing to do with finances. We suspect he is involved in drugs, but we can't prove anything. Not that we are in the business of reporting anything our clients do that isn't exactly above board, it just isn't our business. But this guy, he's pretty slippery if you know what I mean." "What's his name? Has he been in trouble with the law before?" I asked, although I don't know why I asked. It's not like I gave a shit what his name was, or whether he was known to police, I was just asking for the sake of asking. I swear sometimes stuff comes out of my mouth that I am sure belongs to someone else. It's like it's on the tip of my tongue and out of my mouth before I even know it. "Lawrence Farber is his name, and I don't know whether he has a record, or whether the police know anything about him." "Why the heck would the two of them choose a dog park in the middle of the city to have a make out session? Seems pretty juvenile to me," I said. "It's probably Georgette's idea of romantic, who knows what was going on in her empty head," Natasha said.

I left Natasha sitting at her desk staring at the pictures and thinking, at least I think that's what she was doing. She might have been sleeping with her eyes opened for all I knew. She looked mesmerized.

I worked away at my desk, getting ready for the next reception and then got up to take the puppies for their morning gallop through the park. After walking the short distance to the dog park I let the two little darlings free, and I sat on a bench and popped my shoulder back in its socket, and waited while the two of them experienced their joyful romp of freedom.

When I got back to the office there was a big shopping bag on my desk. It had a tag addressed to me hanging from the handle of the shopping bag. I knocked on Natasha's door and when she called answered, I walked in with the shopping bag, "Do you know who left this? I haven't opened it yet but I can't imagine who it is from." "Sorry dear, I haven't a clue. I didn't hear anyone come in when you were out with the dogs. Open it let's take a look shall we." I put the back on her desk and opened it up and pulled out a small Louis Vuitton bag. "Good heavens, a Louis bag." I dug around the shopping bag and found an envelope with a card inside. I opened it up and read the card, 'Please accept this bag as my way of apologizing. I want to be your friend but I haven't got much experience. Georgette.' I had read the card aloud to Natasha. "What'll I do now?" I asked. I didn't want to hang around with Georgette; she wasn't my kind of girlfriend. "You should do what your heart tells you. Now that I know what she is up to, you don't have to put up with her on my account. Lucius and me will figure a way to get the goods on Georgette ourselves, so don't worry on that score." Natasha was right but I still had to give Georgette my answer in terms of whether I would work for her.

There was also Gina to think about. Call me a nosey bugger, but I also wanted to know what and who Gina was after as an undercover cop. I decided that I was going to continue to play snoop for Natasha. "I actually want to continue to help you and Lucius. I need to get in touch with Georgette and thank her for the bag, and maybe I'll meet her for a coffee or something tomorrow. We might even go to the movies. I'll just keep fishing around, and trying to find out what is going on in her little world." "Thank you Siobhan, I appreciate your efforts. Just don't get yourself to involved with Georgette's boyfriend. He's a dangerous guy, so be very careful. On another topic; we need to go over our plans for the Friday reception so let's sit down tomorrow morning after you walk Lola and Coco."

I went back to my desk with my new bag that I wasn't sure I should keep. I wasn't a Georgette fan but I sure don't want her buying me gifts to win me over. After thinking what to say, I decided to call her and ask to meet her tomorrow night for a coffee. I had also decided that I had to give the bag back. She hadn't done anything that wrong. She just rubbed me the wrong way and maybe it was a misunderstanding on my part. Maybe I was being to sensitive. So I dialed her number. She was happy to hear from me so I asked her if she wanted to get together tomorrow night for coffee. She agreed and then asked what I thought of the handbag. I told her I loved it and before I could tell I couldn't possibly keep it she said, "I thought it would help bring your evil looking wardrobe up a couple of notches. Nothing personal but 'really'." So instead of getting angry at her latest dose of verb diarrhea, I said nothing and took off the tags on the bag.

After I hung up I realized that Georgette is truly one of a kind. She doesn't have a clue how to behave, it's like she has no filter whatsoever. I either had to put up with her, and ignore her barbs, or write her off as bad news.

I knew I couldn't explain the bag to my Mom, she would tell me to send it back because it was too expensive, and Georgette was not a nice enough person to spend time with. I decided to tell my Mom that I bought the bag myself, and that it was a knock off Louis Vuitton bag. When I got home I went into the kitchen to show mom the bag.

"That's a nice roomy little bag honey. Was it expensive? It doesn't look it but you never know these days." Mom said. "It was cheap ma, it's a Louis Vuitton knockoff." "Louis who?" She asked. I started to laugh and realized I probably didn't need to make up a story about the bag. Mom didn't have a clue who the designer was, and I'm pretty sure she didn't care who he was. She's a Sears shopper and that's that.

Dinner that night was a back porch picnic. Every so often my Mom decides we need to change eating venues and so she sets up a picnic on the back porch. Most families would go to a restaurant for a change of venue. Our back porch was more of a stoop than a porch and so the whole picnic thing is a tough assignment given the limited real estate the back porch offers. My folks wouldn't dream of putting a large porch on the back of the house because my parents are big time gardeners and don't like to waste space on a sitting area, that's what the living room is for, don'tcha' know. After we finished our porch picnic I helped Mom clean up, and went up to my room to call Marcy. After I told her what went on with the bag and all the Georgette shit she said she'd be right over, which I hoped she say. I waited outside for Marcy, I wanted to tell her what I had told my Mom about the bag. "I knew that before you told me. I would tell my Mom the same thing, so no worries." That's my gal!

Mom and Dad were at the kitchen table having tea and dessert, and asked Marcy and me to join them. How could I refuse my Mom's cherry cheesecake? I couldn't and neither could Marcy so we both hunkered down to a slab of the heavenly confection my Mom calls her 'Cherry Cheesecake Delight', and with a big old whack of whipped cream the culinary delight is complete.

After dessert Marcy and I went up to my room. "Let's see it." I brought out the bag to show her and after a thorough inspection she said, "It's a knockoff." I grabbed the bag off her and looked at it myself trying to see what she saw. "What are you talking about? It can't be a knockoff, it had paperwork and it was in a Louis shopping bag." I said sounding pretty feeble. "Trust me Siobhan, I did my homework when you told me about it. Look I'll show you." She proceeded to point out the stitching and the lining detail that I never noticed. Sure enough after a quick check on the internet it was confirmed, Georgette, the bitch, had given me a friggin' knockoff. After I got over ranting and being pissed off the two of us started to laugh. "Do you think she knows it's a knockoff? Maybe she thinks it's the real McCoy, and she bought it and paid full pop." Marcy said. I gave Marcy a 'you're not serious look'. "No Miss Dipshit knew exactly what she was doing. To think I almost kissed her ass when I thanked her for the bag. I could just vomit right now." Marcy started to laugh, and in a few seconds, yours truly joined in the laugh fest.

Chapter 12

The first thing I did when I got into the office the next morning was track down Natasha, I wanted to tell her about the bag, "I knew it had to be too good to be true, I thanked her profusely, and she actually told me that she bought it because she figured my wardrobe needed help, her actual words 'she thought the bag would bring my evil looking wardrobe up a few notches.'" Natasha was laughing, so was I for that matter. "She never disappoints does she?" "No she doesn't and I'm meeting her tonight for a coffee. I'm trying to decide what I can do to get back at her. I'm not sure what it is yet but I'm definitely going to do something." I said. I went back to my office and checked for messages and, after replying to some of them I took a look at Natasha's schedule. I was working my little heart out and the phone rang. It was Gina, she asked me if I wanted to get together Friday night. I was surprised that she wanted to hang out with me. She seemed strictly business, but I said, "How about Saturday night or Thursday night. I can't make it Friday I'm going out with some friends from school on Friday night." She agreed and said she would meet me at the same bar and we could go from there, whatever that means.

I hung up and felt pretty damn nervous. First of all, I lied to Gina when I told her I was busy on Friday night, and what's scary is

I was a cool as a cucumber when I lied. I'm not sure why I lied, but I think I just wanted to have the upper hand. Dumb attitude I know, but I did it anyway. Like I said, sometimes I think I'm possessed and it's someone else speaking, not me. Now I had two dates this week, Georgette and Gina. I decided not to tell Natasha about my 'date' with Gina on Saturday.

You'll notice in all my outings and 'dates' none of them are with the opposite sex. To be honest I couldn't give a rat's ass about dating a guy, I think it is entirely overrated and way too stressful to be fun. It's always a crap shoot; if he spends a lot of money on the date then you know it's like a bank loan that requires some sort of repayment usually in the form of trying to get beyond 2nd base. If you suggest sharing the expense of an evening out, and he accepts then it's like dating your brother or some cheap jerk you want to toss twenty bucks at and go home. Definitely a crap-shoot. Half the time when I do have a date and it starts out good, it almost always ends up with me checking my watch to see how many more hours I have to listen to Mr. Boring drone on about how good he is at some crap I couldn't care less about. After two dates with the same guy, I can pretty much guarantee that he thinks he's halfway to the big. Where does that come from? It's like a boob squeeze is payment for a latte. I wonder what a burger is worth.

After I took the dogs for their morning romp I knocked on Natasha's door and the two of us sat and talked about the Friday reception. After we finished the meeting Natasha shared my lunch buffet, pork cutlet sandwiches, potato salad and brownies; a light, but nourishing lunch, guaranteed to bring on a wave of sleepiness about two hours after consuming.

I wasn't going to go home first before I met Georgette so I spent the couple of extra hours catching up on some work for Natasha, and I was still trying to decide how to get back at Georgette over the handbag fiasco. I was working away at my desk when Natasha came out of her office, “I have an idea for your ‘get even with Georgette’ challenge.” I looked up and Natasha was holding a bunch of tacky looking flowers, and an equally tacky handbag. “This was part of a costume I wore years ago. I think you should glue the flowers all over the bag, put it in a gift bag and give it to Georgette. What do you think?” I was smiling big time and said, “I love it. I’ll tell her I thought of her the minute I saw this bag, and knew I had to get it for her.” The two of us chuckled together and ‘decorated’ the bag. After stepping back to admire our handiwork I said, “Natasha, this may be a second business. We can call it ‘Bag Lady’ and all we do is create completely ugly bags to give as gifts to people you don’t like.” “You may be onto something. Why do all gifts have to be full of warm sentiment? What’s wrong with giving someone you dislike an ugly gift?” Natasha said. I totally agreed and Georgette will be the recipient of a gift that is completely devoid of beauty and any sort of warm sentiment.

I went to the bathroom and washed my face and put on some makeup. Not that it would have made a whole heap of difference. It was hot out and the minute the heat and sun hit my face a new crop of freckles would pop out on my face, as if someone had phoned the freckle department and ordered a fresh crop of brown dots just for me.

I walked over to the café, with my special gift for Georgette all wrapped and ready for its presentation. Of course, Georgette wasn’t there, nor would she be for another half hour. Once again my fury floated to the surface, and I am seething by the time the dipshit shows up. She sails in and plunks herself down in front of me, and immediately starts calling someone. “You are something else, you bad mannered bitch. You are late, you don’t even say hello or apologize and you immediately start talking on the phone the minute you sit down.” She looks and me rather meekly and says, “Sorry for being late. Do you forgive me?” “Actually, no I don’t. You are inappropriate and unprofessional but that is who you are I suppose. Here I have something for you." I handed her my gift and she opened it and her mouth dropped opened. "Wow, that is totally ugly. Why would you give me something like that? I bought you a Louis bag."

"Actually no you didn't. You bought me a knock off. At first you insulted me by the comment you made about my evil wardrobe, and then you added salt to the wound by giving me a cheap knockoff and pretended it was the real thing. You should be ashamed of yourself."

Georgette sat staring at me for several moments, I guess she was trying to figure out a comeback. "I didn't think you'd notice it was a knockoff. I wanted to give you something and didn't want to buy you the real thing, a real Louis bag would be wasted on you, but I wanted to give you something so I gave you a knockoff. I didn't mean to offend you with my comments. I don't have a filter, I just say what I feel like saying."

The 'wasted on you' remark added to all the other shit she's said is enough to do anyone in but I just sucked it up, and decided to let everything roll along. I didn't like the empty headed pinhead, but I had made a commitment to Natasha, and I would follow through.

"Let's forget all this okay. How is your business going? Have you made any headway yet?" Georgette looked quite surprised at my turnaround. I think she expected me to get up and walk out, but in that moment, when she delivered her second ridiculous insult, I decided to suck it up and do my own Georgette filtering. "Oh, well let me think, I'm hoping to make the move and open the business in a couple of weeks. I've got a list of girls I'm going to talk to about joining me. Do you want to see my list? Maybe you know some of the girls and can give me your ideas about them. You know what I mean, things like – are they cute? – do they have good hair?, stuff like that." I'm sitting and staring at Georgette and I have to blink a couple of times to be sure I'm not in an alternate universe which is populated by good looking morons. "Sure let's see who you have." She handed me her list that had about five names on it. "You only have five girls on your list. How come so short?" I asked. Big eyes like empty saucers looked at me. "Silly, these are just the girls from Natasha's, I've already lined up a bunch of girls from other places that are for sure joining me. They're friends of mine, you know girls I hang out with." I looked down her list again and noticed Gina's name. "I'll let you know about these girls. I just need to connect a name with a face. They'll be at the reception tomorrow, right?" "Yeah, probably they'll be there. It'll be my last reception. I've got some invitations printed that I'm going to secretly hand out to the dishiest and richest guys at the party," she said. "That's not a good idea Georgette. First of all you could get caught and secondly you're telling me, like you think I won't mention anything to Natasha. You really need to practice a little verbal discretion. Drop the idea completely," I said. Once again numb nuts stared at me with vacuous saucer like eyes. "What do you mean? Would you tell Natasha? I thought we had a deal." "I never said we had a deal. You have barely told me anything about your new business. No, I won't tell Natasha, but you absolutely cannot do that. It's tacky and besides any guy with class would toss out your invite without even looking at it. You want to run a classy place right? Handing out flyers isn't classy." Georgette was getting a little antsy. I guess focusing on one thing for too long makes her lose her concentration. YIKES. "Maybe you're right. If I got caught it would be totally embarrassing. The guys I want as clients I can find a way of getting in touch with anyway. Thanks for that. I can't tell you anything until we open up. My partners don't want me talking about it. They don't know I told you, but I had to tell someone even if it was just you." There goes her unfiltered gob again.

After another twenty minutes of Georgette's droning on about eyebrow waxing, moisturizers and the genetic marvel that is her perfect body, we left the café. I personally felt like I'd just done ten rounds with a heavyweight boxer.

When I got home I had tea and cookies with my folks and then went up to my room and flopped into my bed. I slept like a baby and got up ready to take on the day.

Chapter 13

The next morning after a behemoth breakfast, I left for work. Why the big breakfast, considering I'm trying to be more body conscious? The fact is, I went to bed without dinner, and my body needs the fuel, sorry but that's just the way it is. Lucius was outside waiting for me. "Hi what are you doing here?" I said as I climbed into the car. "Natasha wanted me to take you to the hairdresser first before you start your day. It's going to be pretty busy and you won't have time to do your hair later."

The whole drive I'm thinking to myself, 'I hope the hairdresser knows what he or she is doing. They'll probably shit when they see my crowning 'gory'.' When we got to the salon and my hair washed and conditioned I sat and thought about what I would tell Natasha. I was beginning to feel caught in the middle – beginning, end, who am I kidding I was beginning to feel like a UN Ambassador. I asked myself, why the hell had I agreed to do this in first place? One thing was for sure whatever I decided to tell Natasha would be the edited version. I also had to decide if I would mention anything to Gina about being on Georgette's list of possibles. By the time I had finished my mental wresting match my hair was done, and I looked like a million bucks, although the pouf on the top of my head was a tad pronounced, I still looked pretty damn good.

I got back to the office, and once again both my office and Natasha's were awash in cocktail dresses, makeup artists and girls. I went out to the reception area to check on the bar and catering as well as flowers and I spotted Natasha in deep conversation with Lucius. She looked up and spotted me, and then waved me over. "How was your evening with Georgette? Did she like you little gift?" Natasha said. I smiled and said, "She didn't get why I would buy her anything so tasteless. When I confronted her about the knockoff she said she didn't want to waste money on someone who wouldn't appreciate it." Natasha's look of shock was quite funny. "She is a piece of work. She never disappoints, that's for sure. She actually said that to you?" "That and more, but after she told me she didn't have a verbal filter, I decided to develop my own for everything that Georgette said to me that was uncouth and ignorant," I said. I had decided that I would tell Natasha very little about the conversation I had with Georgette. I told her I would fill her in on the details later.

The reception went off without a hitch and by nine o'clock we were locking up. I spotted Georgette chatting up the same Romeo I saw her with in the park. Lucius drove me home and I was very happy for the lift. Standing around smiling like an ape for several hours wore me out.

When I got home I called Marcy to tell her about my day. When she answered the phone I realized someone was with her. She excused herself and a few seconds later she said, "Shiv, I'm on a date. Seriously a date with a cute guy I met at the library. It's not actually a date, date, but I like him and we'll see. Come over to my place tomorrow morning and I'll tell you all about it. Got to go." I hadn't gotten a word in edge wise before she hung up. I was actually kind of glad because I know if she wasn't on a date she would have wanted to come over, and I was way too baffled to do any sort of entertaining, even if it was just Marcy.

I went to the living room and had a cup of tea and a slice of cake and told my parents about my day. “Your Aunt Bertie and Uncle Ron are coming over tomorrow and staying the night. Will you be around?” Mom said. I told them I would be at Marcy’s for a while then I was meeting someone from work tomorrow night. I didn’t tell them who but I said she was a new friend and we were just going to have a coffee together.

My Aunt Bertie is a total character. She’s more than a bit on the tubby side and with good reason. She loves her food. She loves to cook it, share it and eat it. When she’s not cooking or eating she’s laughing at your jokes, her jokes and jokes she just remembered. She never walks anywhere, she does a sort of march-type run all the while humming to some tune that’s embedded in her brain. She starts planning what she’s going to cook for each meal, one meal in advance. So her breakfast is always decided at dinner the night before. Her lunch is sorted out at breakfast and her dinner designed at lunch. In between there’s the snack quotient of the days groceries to consider, and so she factors that into her breakfast to lunch and her lunch to dinner meal planning. My mom and her sister Bertie get on like a house on fire. They finish each other’s sentences, and laugh until they cry over the silliest things. I could easily sit and listen to them all day long. I was kind of bummed that I was going to be out for part of the visit. “I’ll be around later Saturday and all day Sunday.” I said. “That’s great honey. I’ve been cooking all day, so go grab yourself something to eat if you’re hungry.” I had just finished eating a slice of cake the size of a midsize car, so hunger wasn’t an issue with me. “No thanks ma, I’m off to bed.”

Chapter 14

The next morning I got up and went for a run. I know, I can hardly stand myself I'm getting so friggin' fit. When I got back Mom thought I should have a nap after all that exertion, but instead I had a shower and then partook of the Saturday Murphy Family Breakfast Buffet. After consuming my weight in home fries and bacon I pushed myself away from the table, undid the top button of my jeans, and waddled up to my room. I debated having a lay down if for no other reason but to redistribute the wodge of carbs I had lying on my gut. Instead I brushed my teeth, changed into shorts and a top and sandals, and then called Marcy.

I wanted to know about the so-called 'date' she had gone on, and find out what time we were meeting. Marcy answered after the first ring, must have been a hell of a date, "What time do you want to meet?" I said. "Come on over to my place in an hour. I have to tell you about last night." I hung up and went into the bathroom and washed my face and pulled a comb through my hair. I decided to walk to Marcy's place, hoping to wear off a few calories on the way, and after another cup of coffee with my folks, I sailed out the door.

Marcy's folks and mine are pretty much the same type of people, hardworking, and just plain nice. Not that being nice is plain, if you get my drift. Her Mom works in the bank and her Dad owns a picture-framing store. He wants Marcy to take over the family business, as if. Marcy helps out in the store whenever she can, but she got a summer job at the library this year, which is a big deal in terms of independence. Every summer in the past she has worked at the shop with her dad, so finding the job at the library was huge. Her Dad was disappointed but I think he understood. Her next challenge is going to be telling her folks that her future isn't in picture framing. Marcy is interested in studying law enforcement. She wants to study forensic science or something like that. We don't spend a lot of time discussing career paths and all that crap.

Marcy's house is definitely designed for comfort. The living room is like a temple, dedicated to the television god, big comfy loungers, a massive mother of a sofa, and TV trays everywhere. Their dining room is like a storage area. The table is stacked with magazines, books, bags and china. Food comes out of the kitchen, bypasses the dining room, and lands on the TV trays. All conversation takes place during commercials. They have their shows, and watching them is almost a religious experience. Marcy doesn't worship at the TV temple, she eats in the kitchen or her room. Even though it sounds like a dysfunctional type family unit, it isn't at all. Marcy has an older brother who, in order to dodge picture framing business bullet, moved to another state, leaving Marcy the 'it' girl when it comes to the picture framing dynasty and all it entails.

After the usual hellos and offers of tea, coffee, soft drinks, and the lower half of the fridge, Marcy and me went up to her room. "So, spill. What's with the date? I didn't even know there was anybody cute at the library." "Trust me, there isn't. I had a temporary lapse in judgment. I wasted an evening and had to fight off a friggin' octopus who figured he bought me a coffee and a cookie, and that entitled him to cop a feel," Marcy said. "You've got to be kidding. He actually tried to grab a boob after 'not really a date' date?" I said. "Yes, but trust me he won't be grabbing anyone anytime soon. I think I broke his jaw when I hit him." "You hit him? For real you actually hauled off and decked him. That's hysterical," I said. "Upper cut to the jaw, followed by a good stomping on his foot with my size sevens." I just about peed my pants laughing at the visual. The hapless smuck will pay for the actions of his wandering hands for a long time to come. Don't ever mess with Marcy. My own experience with the male population has been about as successful as Marcy's. It's not like the two of us have really high standards, and need to be wined and dined or anything like that, but finding a guy who is normal, and not twitchy, iffy or weird is pretty tough. I'm sure there are lots of guys who think Marcy and me are twitchy, iffy and weird.

"I have a lot to tell you about what's going on at the office. I've been storing up a whole lot of stuff and I've been dying to tell you. First of all you remember the fake bag thing." I said. "Yeah, whatever happened, did you say something to her?" I told Marcy about showing Natasha the bag and then what we put together to give to her. "I love it! What did she say? Did she get it or did she just think you had incredibly bad taste?" "She actually didn't understand how I could give her something so ugly after she had given me a Louis bag. That's when I told her that I knew it was a knockoff and you'll never guess what she said. Okay I'll tell you, she said she didn't think it was worth wasting money on the real thing for someone like me," I said. Marcy looked like she was going to explode, I actually saw smoke coming out of her ears. "That does it, where does this bitch live? I'm going over there right now and knock the shit out of her. Seriously she needs to have her ass kicked, and I'm the gal to do it. How did you not slap her silly?" Marcy said. "Trust me I came very close, but I decided to take the high road and let it roll off me. She's a brainless twit, and I don't want to waste any energy on being mad at her. Besides I like the whole Sherlock Holmes detective thing I'm doing right now, and drop kicking her would probably put an end to it."

I told Marcy about showing Natasha the picture I took of Georgette and her gigolo. "I cropped out the picture of Gina before I showed it to Natasha. I figured I wanted to keep that information to myself, at least for now anyway."

"So what are you going to do about Gina? What do you think she's looking for?" Marcy asked. "At this point I haven't the foggiest. Natasha told me that Georgette's guy was a real dangerous dude, so I'm wondering if he's Gina's target or at least part of it." "It's got to be more than just him. I think she's checking the whole place out. Could be a friggin' drug ring or blackmail deal, you never know." We both sat chewing on the whole thing and I remember thinking this is way more fun than anything we did last summer.

"I'm going to be seeing Gina tonight, which should be interesting. Do you think I should tell her that she's on Georgette's list of recruits? I'm wondering if I should tell her all about Georgette, and her plans and the guy she was kissing and all that stuff. What do you think?" I asked. "You told Gina you'd keep her in the loop right? If you heard anything interesting or weird so maybe you should be straight with her. That's what I would do. Don't tell her anything about Natasha or you could blow your job. In the meantime we need to find out more about her charity shit, so I'm going full out on my detective work next week. I'm going to find out everything I can about Natasha and her paramour Lucius. I'm also going to find out whether Gina is who she says she is," Marcy said. I love Marcy when she's got something to do, a project or whatever, she's like a dog with a bone.

We both went to the living room to join the TV tray set and socialize for a while. I actually have my own tray, ready whenever I need it. Marcy's Mom doesn't create quite the volume of food my

Mom does, but her attitude towards eating is pretty much the same. The two of them – maybe it's a generational thing and all women that age are the same – they both believe that there should always be some sort of food at the ready all the time, just in case.

After talking with Marcy's parents for a half hour or so I got up to leave. Marcy walked me to the door, "Let me know how it goes with this Gina babe. Call me, if it's not too late and we can meet for coffee, or we can get together tomorrow." I said I would, and I headed off home to get changed and meet Gina.

Aunt Bertie was in the kitchen with my folks eating a slice of pie. Of course, they're eating, what else would they be doing? Chanting or reading the bible, I think not. Pie, any kind of sweet pie, is my Mom's version of an appetizer. "Dinner will be ready in about an hour dear." Mom said as I poked my head in the room to announce my return. "I'm just going to change my clothes and I'll be right back." I wanted to spend some time with Aunt Bertie and the best place to do that is around the kitchen table. Eating is the same as pump priming to Aunt Bertie. By the time she's finished whatever is on her plate, she's got a full head of steam, and she's ready to go.

I raced upstairs and stood in front of my closet staring at my pathetic excuse for a wardrobe. Finally I decided on a pair of jeans and a shirt. I put on some sandals, earrings and a bracelet scrubbed my face and applied an unfortunate shade of peach to my lips. On a fluffy blond with a perfect complexion the peach would look wonderful, not so much on my freckle splattered face. I had bought the shade after the first reception at Natasha's. The makeup artist used a peach color on my lips and it looked great. What do I know about 'shades' I figured 'peach was peach', so I grabbed the first and cheapest peach lipstick I found. It looked like crap, kind of pukey, but I paid for it and I was going to wear it. Besides it wears off and then the color isn't nearly as bad.

After spending the next hour or so with my folks and my Aunt I left for to meet Gina. I got to the bar about ten minutes early and found a table in the corner. I'm sitting at my table minding my own business when some creepy jackass of a guy comes over and asks if he can join me. He sits down opposite me before I can even answer. "I'm waiting for someone so, no you can't join me." He sat and stared at me like I was speaking Martian, and he never moved. I said, "Someone is joining me, please leave." The freak is still staring and that's when I realize he is hammered, as in totally wasted. After staring at me for a few more seconds his eyes seemed to cross and he pitches forward and lands face down on the table grinning the whole while. "You're kinda cute, weird hair but cute," he blabs. Great, I'm getting a back hand compliment from a piss tank, who is now not only lying face down on the table top but he has some sort of goobery gob shite coming out of his mouth. I am now utterly grossed out and just as I'm about to get up and look for another table Gina shows up. "Hey Siobhan who's your friend?" I start to answer and lickety split Gina grabs Mister Boozy Ass by the back of his shirt, drags him out of the booth and then literally throws him out the door of the bar. A bunch of the guys at the bar turned around to watch her and then gave her a round of applause, she bowed and then came over to the booth. I'm sitting there with my mouth hanging open, "You have to show me how you do that. That was awesome, you could be a body guard for some famous person and make a fortune." I said that last bit then thought what the hell am I some kind of Pollyanna A-hole or something. Gina just laughed, "You get to learn a thing or two being a cop. So how is everything in the world of Natasha and company?" After we both ordered a drink I gave her a rundown on the goings on. I had decided to tell almost everything in the hopes she would be straight with me. "You mean that bubblehead Georgette wants me to join her posse?" I told her about Georgette wanting me to come on board as well. I still hadn't told Gina about what I was doing for Natasha, the whole snooping around business. "Are you going to accept her offer?" Gina asked. "You've got to be joking. I wouldn't in a million years, but I want to find out more about what she or rather her partners are planning. I think it's something else other than escorting," I said. Gina sat staring at me for a couple of seconds, "You're right it is. I'll get crucified if anyone finds out I'm telling you this but you're already in it and you know something is going on so I'll tell you." I'm sitting in the booth on edge of my seat and I'm about to crap myself I'm so nervous, "Tell me what? Spill before I have or coronary or an ass explosion, I'm so nervous." Gina started to laugh and of course I joined her and then after she had calmed down she said, "We've been watching the whole organization for quite a while. It isn't about escorts and a little hanky panky on the side, that's small potatoes. I know there's some sort of blackmail going on and maybe some drugs are involved. Right now I'm just putting it all together. The more I dig, the deeper it gets and now I'm being told to back off by my boss who is being told by his boss." "I don't think Natasha is involved in any blackmail business. She uses her clients to support her charities, but it's pretty above board. I write the letters so I know the tone and language she uses." Gina sat with a bit of a smile on her face. "I know it isn't Natasha, but if I tell you who I think it is you are going to have to swear on a friggin' stack of bibles you will keep shut about it, do you swear?" After nodding like a bobble head doll Gina blurts out, "I'm pretty sure it's Lucius." "Lucius? It can't be he is so loyal to Natasha, he wouldn't jeopardize her or her business, no way no how," I said. "How can you be so sure?" I knew I had told Natasha that I would keep her and Lucius's relationship quiet, I felt I had to tell Gina. She was a cop after all. "They used to be married for crap sake. He is still in love with her, I know it, I can tell how he looks at her." What a jerk I am, I sounded like the president of the

Lucius fan club. "Did they tell you to keep it to yourself?" I nodded, "Yes, and I feel bad telling you after I promised to keep quiet about it." "Don't feel bad, the two of them tell everyone the same thing. It kind of makes them look like star crossed lovers or some shit like that. In reality they are anything but great friends. It's true they were married but she dropped him for a richer guy six months after they got hitched. After she married this new guy Lucius came back, down on his luck, and Natasha gave him a job. In the meantime her new guy up and drops dead of a heart attack, and she inherits a pantload of money, a townhouse, condo and a home in the Hamptons. Not a bad day's work for gal from the Bronx." I staring at her with my mouth wide-open like I'm catching flies, "Are you serious? I don't know where I thought she got the money. I suppose I thought she was some member of European royalty who immigrated here to live her life in quiet splendor, doing good deeds and all that." I said. "European royalty, that's rich. Nope Natasha is just an ordinary run to the mill home grown kind of gal. She was a real looker when she was young, and pretty ambitious to boot. She's got a big heart and basically she is an honest person. Like I said she's not my target, it's Lucius. He's a nasty piece of shit, and he's using Natasha and her contacts to get fodder for his blackmailing business. I still don't know about the drug part of what is going on there but I intend on finding out. I could use some help from you. What do you say?" I felt totally in the center of this whole thing. On the one hand I had an even bigger reason than before to be loyal to Natasha. Lucius was a danger to her and I didn't want anything to happen to her. Gina was a cop and my sense of right and wrong, and civic duty kept flashing before my eyes. I wanted to help and Gina as well as look out for Natasha. "Sure I'll help. I don't know what I can do and I sure don't want to get caught snooping, so if you can figure out what you want me to do that doesn't involve getting caught with my hand in the cookie jar then I'm in."

Gina nodded with approval and for the next half hour or so we talked about how I can help. First off I was just going to watch and report to Gina. I told her I was going to egg Georgette on a bit and see where it goes, and she agreed.

Who knew a summer job could be this great? I felt like I was in a movie, it's totally unreal. Of course, not for a second did I think it could possibly be dangerous. Why would it be? All I was planning on doing was watching and reporting, nothing more dangerous than that. I was also going to keep a hairy eyeball on Lucius the friggin' leper.

I wanted to tell Natasha to watch out for Lucius, but I needed to figure out the best way to broach the subject. It's not something you blurt out, or bring up over a cup of tea, "Oh, Natasha you know that guy Lucius that hangs around with you all the time, the one you've known for a million years, anyway the guy is a total prick and he is out to screw you big time," hmm tactful, but perhaps a bit too straight to the point, maybe a more subtle approach would be appropriate

Chapter 15

I spent a good part of Sunday sitting at the kitchen table with my Mom and Aunt Bertie. I never knew I could drink that much tea or eat that many cookies. I swear the cookies come to the table on a conveyor belt. By the end of the afternoon I was ready for a nap. I was teaed, cookied and talked out. I left the two Olympic chatterboxes at the table and went upstairs to my room. I thought I would spend a bit of time researching Natasha again and her elusive Rhode Island Charity. After a couple of hours and zero results my Mom called up to me to tell me Aunt Bertie was leaving. After going down for my bear hug and then my promise to visit as soon as I could, I went to the living room to flop in front of the TV with my folks. Mom likes to regurgitate every last detail of a visit. What is that anyway? Is it a family trait? If it is, shoot me now, before I catch it. It drives my Dad and me and nuts, but what the heck, that's my Mom and who knows I may end up being just like her.

I went up to my room messed around for a while then hit the hay. I wanted to get up early and walk at least part way to work. I had about fifteen thousand cookies to work off. After shoveling down a breakfast I left the house. I stepped outside just as Lucius pulled up in the limo. I was thinking crap, now that I know what this guy is all about I don't want to be alone with him. I wanted to at least work out how I'm going to act in front of him. I'm not real good at being deceptive; my face is like a big old open book. I decided to slap on a big smile and my sunglasses and climbed into the limo. "We're meeting Natasha at Saks, I take it you've had your breakfast?" "You know it." I said and then looked out the window trying to give the air of quiet contemplation. What an a-hole I am, quiet contemplation, I was bursting to take a run at Lucy, that's my new name for the prick. Maturity kicked in and after one minute of staring out, I unloaded a string of long pointless stories designed to bore the poop out of anyone within earshot. It's a technique I learned at Aunt Bettie's feet.

When we got to Saks Natasha was waiting on the sidewalk and after loading up we went around doing her Monday shopping and appointments, all the while chatting about her next charity event that was coming up.

We got to the office and I immediately took the beasts for a gallop. I can't imagine what would happen if they had an 'accident' in the brownstone. We'd have to shut down the place down for repairs. Anyway once I got back and popped by arm back into its socket, I grabbed my lunch and decided to eat it at my desk. Halfway through round one of my smorgasbord of a meal Georgette walked in. She took one look at my feast and said, "No wonder you're such a tubby, look at the size of your lunch. Didn't anyone tell you that kind of food goes right on your ass?" Instead of blowing my cool and drop kicking the stupid bitch, I just kept on eating and working. "Do you want something Georgette, or did you come over here to shoot your unfiltered mouth off?" I said. "Well it's true, you shouldn't eat that much food at one sitting. Anyway, I wanted to know if you had time to get together tomorrow night. I have a date type thing tonight so tomorrow I'm free. Let's meet at a restaurant instead of the café, that way we can have dinner, and I'll show you what you should be eating. How's that sound?" I wanted to yell at her and call her every nasty name I could think of and then shove the rest of my meatball sandwich up her pert ass, but I decided to chill and said, "Sounds like a plan. How about Vesuvio's at seven? Oh, and if you just once tell me how and what to eat I'll plow you, got it?" Georgette giggled and then swished out the door. I swear she is the biggest jackass jerk I have ever met.

After she left the office Natasha came in and asked me to join her in her office. "Siobhan, how are things, I noticed Georgette in the lobby. Was she in to see me or you?"

"Me, aren't I the lucky one? She wants to get together tomorrow night for dinner. I have a feeling she wants me to meet her investors or at least talk about them. I gotta tell you though, for two pins I would have drop kicked her today. She has no off switch or filter." Natasha was laughing, "You have a way with words. If you do decide to drop kick her, give me a heads up, I would love to see that. Are you going?" "I'm going to go if for no other reason than to bask in her ridiculous light. She is breathtaking in her stupidity, so much so I actually feel sorry for her," I said. "Don't waste your pity. I've had phone calls from some of my best clients. Apparently Georgette has been doing quite a bit of promotional work on her new business. I think I'm going to let her go. I can't have her playing fast and loose with my business." Natasha said. "Are you sure you want to do that before you have an idea of what's going on? Give me another week before you do anything. I want to find out more about what she has in mind, which probably isn't too much considering her minuscule brain." I said. Natasha stared for a couple of seconds and then said, "Okay, but be really careful and if you meet or have any contact with that guy of hers run the other way. He's bad news. I really mean that, he is scary and dangerous as far as I'm concerned. Let me know what happens tomorrow night. And again you be careful."

I went back to my desk and finished off the work I had.

Thursday night was a fundraiser and I had to coordinate things with the event planners so I needed to make a list of questions I needed answers to.

At the end of the day I went in to say goodbye to Natasha and then walked to the subway. I got off a couple of stops early to get in some exercise. I decided to give Gina a call when I got home. I was also going to talk to Marcy. Halfway home I remembered it was Zumba night so I stopped at my favorite bakery for a couple of brownies. What, I needed sustenance; it was going to be a long night. I called Gina on my cell and told her about my get together with Georgette tomorrow night. She asked me to let her know what Georgette had to say and then hung up.

I got home and after ten minutes of explaining to my mom why I didn't need a fifteen-course meal before I worked out, I left to meet Marcy.

Chapter 16

When I got to the office the next day there was a big pile of paper and files on my desk. I sat behind my desk and reached for the file on top, and just as I opened it Natasha came into the office and came up to my desk, "Sorry Siobhan, you don't need to worry about these files, I just left them there for a second and forgot about them. I'll look after them," and she picked up the pile and walked to her office. I still had the first file in front of me. I was about to bring it into Natasha when I noticed the name on the file "Rhode Island Commemorative Charity. I thought about giving it to Natasha about a nano second and then put it in my handbag instead. I am such a devious, nosy parker.

Natasha called me into her office to discuss the upcoming charity event, "Siobhan, here is a list of things I need you to organize for me. We also need to develop the look and feel of the program, and once again hustle around for silent auction items. I've made a list of places for you to call and get some good items. The items should be top quality expensive merchandise and services, nothing cheap." We sat talking about the event for about an hour and then I reminded her about my 'date' with Georgette. "So what do you think she wants to talk about?" Natasha asked. "It could be anything. Who knows she might just want to talk about what to wear for fall. I think she probably wants to tell me about her business. I have a feeling her beau will show up, but I could be wrong. Whatever happens she will for sure, insult me or put her foot in her mouth somehow, and I almost look forward to her doing it. I know that sounds sick but I'm curious to see just exactly how rude she can be. It's going to take me a lot of willpower not to put my foot up her butt." Natasha was laughing and said, "I would love to be in the room, in disguise if and when you do that."

I took Lola and Coco for their trot, and after they'd both ran around like crazy at the off leash dog park, then they both had a gigantic crap that Mr. Shit Wrangler picked up, and then two happy dogs dragged me back to the office. I started on my silent auction round up and within no time it was lunch and I decided to eat it at my desk. I can't go too much past noon without refueling. It's like I have an alarm clock in my gut. Sad but true. I guess it means I will never be a super model. Drats.

I worked solidly through the afternoon and before I knew it the day was over. I poked my head into Natasha's office to say goodbye and then left to go home and change clothes for my evening with Georgie girl. I wasn't sure what to wear for my big dinner date, whatever I chose, I was pretty sure Georgette would have a comment to make on my choice. Such a stupid meathead.

I got home, and after checking in with my folks, I went up to my room to get ready. I put on a pair of my good trousers, a shirt and a jacket. I changed my shoes and after applying a modest amount of makeup, like I would know what a modest amount of makeup is, I grabbed my purse and after saying goodbye to my parents I left for the restaurant.

On the way to the restaurant I was mentally preparing myself for the encounter. I decided that if she made me wait more than ten minutes I was going to leave. If she insulted me more than once I would empty the contents of my plate on her head, and if she answered her phone or used her phone outgoing I would grab it off of her and hurl it.

When I got to the restaurant Georgette was already at the table, and waved me over when I walked in. “Siobhan, I’m so glad you could make it. You look great.” Yikes, someone broke into her head and stole her brain replacing it with a human brain. “Thanks, you look nice as well.” I sat down, and after some light, one-sided, ‘aren’t I just about the prettiest thing you have ever met’ conversation, we ordered our dinner. I exercised an incredible about of self-control by ordering a light dinner. I knew there’d be some chow at home if I still felt hungry later on. After we finished eating I sat and waited for Georgette to launch into some sort of reason or rationale for why we got together. I have to tell you that unless I am totally engaged in a conversation I tend to have the attention span of a gnat. I must have gone to the bathroom three times. Georgette must have thought I was doing drugs in the can. Finally, after more time spent on long pointless stories than I have been subjected to in a long time, she opened up about the reason for the dinner. “I wanted to meet with you to talk about my business ideas. I trust you and your judgment. You’re smart and I’m just beautiful. My partners are becoming bullies, and don’t talk to me or ask my opinion on things. I want you to talk to them with me and for me. What do you think? Will you do it for me? There are no strings attached or anything like that. You don’t have to come to work for me, or anything like that. I just need someone on my team, on my side.” I was thunderstruck, not that anything she said was revolutionary, but it was the way she said it. Except for the ‘you’re smart and I’m just beautiful’ remark it sounded like something an intelligent human would say. I had to think about things for about ten seconds and then said, “I’ll be happy to help you as long as none of what I do gets back to Natasha.” Georgette’s face lit right up and she nodded like a bobble head. She actually looked pretty ridiculous and a small obnoxious cheer went up in my mind. "Perfect, I promise it will be totally confidential and Natasha will never find out anything. I'm going to tell my partners that you are my assistant and it is important that you're included in all future decisions an' discussions." Once again, a human response, for sure someone absconded with her brain and replaced it with a moderately more intelligent one.

We ordered coffee and as I was about to scoop sugar into my cup Georgette said, "Oh don't do that your skin is already full of spots, sugar is only going to make it worse." Just as I thought things were different who ever kidnapped her brain sent it back. I tossed down some money and stood up to leave, "On that note call when you need me. Have a nice night." And I walked out. Miss Fluffo didn't even wince, she sat with her phone in her ear laughing at whatever the knucklehead at the other end of the call was saying.

I took the subway home and by the time I opened the door I had decided not to tell Natasha anything. I was going to see how it played out. The only person who I was going to tell all to was Marcy.

I got home and filled the empty spots in my stomach with a hunk of chocolate cake the size of a concrete block. There's nothing like hitting the hay with a whacking great load of carbs to lull you to sleep.

Chapter 17

The next day I had decided to get in touch with Marcy so the two of us could go over everything that was going on. As soon I got to the office and barely seated Natasha came out to ask me how my dinner was. I lied, I'm getting pretty good at it, and told her, "It was an evening dedicated to the beauty who is Georgette. Obviously she hates to spend time by herself and I guess, for want of real friends to have dinner with her, she called me. It was a total waste of my time." Natasha chuckled and walked back to her office. I worked away for a couple of hours and then after walking the dogs and taking some calls, Gina called. I had forgotten that I told her about my get together with Georgette. Boy, my social life was becoming a matter of public record. I told her basically exactly what I had told Natasha. I think she was disappointed and I also think that she felt I was holding out on her. Tough butt.

By the end of the day I had gotten in touch with Marcy and the two of us were going to get together at my place for dinner and then I could tell her all about what was going on. I wanted to get her read on everything. Something was bugging me and I wasn't sure what it was.

Marcy, my folks me and had great time at dinner, talking and joking around, Marcy gets along with everybody, unlike yours truly. After helping with the cleanup and loading the dishwasher Marcy and I went up to my room.

I hadn't had a chance to check out the 'Rhode Island' file so I brought that out and we both talked about the whole situation. "Have you got a picture of this Gina babe? Like I said I want to find out if she is who she says she is. I think I should talk to my uncle the cop and see if she's legit. He will check up and see if anyone like her is a cop. Who knows, she might be up to her eyeballs in bullshit and she's stringing you along." "I hadn't thought about it that way, Gina is pretty slick I must admit. I think I can get a picture of her and I'll send it to you. With Georgette, I don't know how guilty she is, I think her partners are into something totally illegal but she isn't. What about Lucius? Gina told me he was her target. What's that all about? Between Georgette, Gina, Lucius and who the hell else I'm totally not trusting anyone except you anymore. You are the only person I'm going to be straight with. I think something is going on but I don't know what. I also think a lot of different factions are involved. This is way too much for my brain."

The two of us sat for a while and went over the file that I had snuck out of the office. Marcy is good at reading complicated documents, and this file was loaded with complicated documents. "I think this Rhode Island Charity thingee is a shell company. There isn't anything in here about what the charity is all about." Marcy said. "Maybe that's why I couldn't find anything about it. Why would Natasha need a shell company? Would she use it to hide money or is it a registered name that she planned on using as a charity later?" I said. "It could be but I doubt it. It hasn't been dormant. This file doesn't have any banking info but it seems pretty current. Things are going on in this company judging by the dates on some of these letters. I can't say for sure but this company is a bit stinky." I started to laugh. I had a vision of Marcy standing up in court and solemnly proclaiming the charity was a bit stinky.

"I'm definitely going to be like totally not saying anything to anyone. I will be very vague from now on. I don't trust anyone. I'm interested to see if Gina is actually a cop. Now that you suggest checking her out I have a feeling she isn't what she seems, and that's kind of scary. She is one tough cookie and I sure as hell don't want to ever mess with her." After talking for a bit longer I walked Marcy to the door and she went home.

I sat in the living room with my parents and had some tea before hitting the old fartsack. Every time I use that word I laugh. Fartsack, I'm such an ass.

Chapter 18

The next day at work it was busy but I got a lot accomplished. I managed to secure a ton of great silent auction items, worked out the program details so the designer could do her thing and drafted a welcome speech for Natasha. One good thing about this job, it was never dull.

I tracked down a picture of Gina and forwarded it to Marcy. I also sent her a picture of Lucius and one of Georgette. Maybe there was something her uncle could dig up about them. Georgette was a non-starter but Lucius, there was something about him that I didn't trust. I couldn't see how he could go from husband and partner to limo driver and not have a burr up his butt or something going on. He just didn't strike me as the kind of person who would be okay with that. He was unsavory – shit I sound like Marcy now.

Halfway through the day Natasha came to get me, and the two of us went to the venue for the next event. In the car Natasha asked me if I had seen the file that I had lifted from the pile she had dropped on my desk. I gulped a bit and then told her I hadn't seen it. Anyway I asked her to describe the file and contents and said I would have a look for it. She said, "It's a file of a shell corporation that Lucius set up. It's dormant now but I need to take a look at it and decide what to do with the company." I sat there thinking if she knew that it was an active company, according to Marcy anyway, why would she say it was inactive and something Lucius set up. "I'll have a look around the office tomorrow. I haven't seen it but it could be anywhere. I'll find it if it's anywhere in the office."

For the rest of the day I was wondering what I was going to do. Should I give Natasha the file and let the chips fall where they may, or should I tell her I can't find it. I decided to call Marcy and drop by her house after work.

I finished off my work and then left the office. I didn't even say goodbye to Natasha. She was in her office with Lucius and I don't think I could have looked him in the eye. I walked to Marcy's place and by the time I got there her mom and dad were ensconced in front of the TV and Marcy had dinner ready for us in the kitchen. I can't imagine chowing down while watching Jerry Springer. I don't know what kind of effect the show would have on my digestive track.

I told Marcy we should wait until we were in her room before we talk about the shenanigans going on at my office. After gulping down dinner the two of us went to her room. "What's going on you sounded in a panic on the phone." I told Marcy about the file and what Natasha said about it being dormant. "Are you sure it's an active file? Maybe it's what Natasha thinks it is," I said. "It's active alright. Did you bring it with you? I'll show you what I mean." I had brought the file so I took it out of my purse and gave it to her. Marcy opened it up and said, "Look, see the dates, some of them are as recent as a month ago. What I don't get is if this Lucius dude is fiddling, why leave the file around for anyone to find." "I don't know who left the files on my desk. I found them there when I went into work. It could have been Lucius who left them lying around. He may have forgotten he had left them there. I don't have the answers, but if Natasha sees that file she is going to blow a gasket, I'm sure," I said. "So what are you going to do? If you want my advice I'd give the file to her and sit back and watch the fireworks." I thought about it for a few minutes and decided that I was going to 'find' the file tomorrow and give it to Natasha. "Any word on the Gina thing?" I asked. "I called my uncle and sent him the pictures you sent me. He said he'd get back to me tomorrow or the next day," Marcy said. After talking for a while longer I said goodbye to her mom and dad and walked home.

I was really tired by the time I got home. Drained I think is a good word for how I felt. I joined my parents in the living room and Mom brought me a cup of her car oil coffee. "Here ya go honey this'll put hair on your chest." Why I'd want hair on my chest is a mystery to me. I loaded the coffee with a shovel full of sugar and gulped it down.

You would think coffee that strong would keep me awake but it has the opposite effect. It's like a mega sleeping pill. Once my head hit the pillow I was out like a light.

Chapter 19

I set my clock for earlier than usual. I wanted to get to work before anyone else and plant the file that Natasha was looking for. I decided that there was nothing else I could do and besides I wanted her to see what was going on. Maybe she knew it and maybe not.

I took the subway all the way into work and used my key to open the front door and just as I was about to disarm the alarm I realized it was already off. Someone else was in the building. Shitty crap, crap. I crept slowly through the lobby to my office, opened the door and cautiously peered in. I don't know why I'm acting like I'm in some mystery movie, creeping along, ducking down, hiding and all that sort of sleuthy type stuff. If anyone sees me I'll say I had stuff to do, and wanted to get an early start on it. Thinking it though, didn't stop me from doing my cat burglar routine. When I got into my office I put my bag in the drawer and noticed that Natasha's office door was opened. Nothing unusual in that and it actually made it easier for me. I didn't have to open her door and freak about the creak it makes. I took the file from my purse and walked into her office and put it on her desk. I was going to tell her that I had found it buried under a pile of correspondence. I dropped the file off and was returning to my desk when I heard the office door turn. I raced to my desk and hid underneath it. Don't ask me why. I am such an A-hole but I figured it had to be something weird because it was barely seven thirty.

I am crouched down and hear two voices, and I strain to hear what they're saying and whom they are. After a few seconds I realize that it was Gina and Lucius. Holy shit, the two of them are up to their eyeballs in something. I can hear Lucius say, "It's an ordinary file with a title tab, "The Rhode Island Commemorative Charity" written on the top. Ah here it is." I couldn't hear anything else and sat crouched and motionless for another couple of minutes before I heard them leave the office. I waited another five minutes under the desk just in case they came back, and then got up and went into Natasha's office. The file was still where I left it but when I opened it up there was nothing in it but a couple of memos with old dates on them. Nothing like Marcy had shown me the night before. They had removed all the original paperwork and replaced the paperwork with old memos and letters.

After I realized that the file had been replaced I needed to go somewhere to think. I decided to go to the café around the corner and have some coffee and sit and think things through. I was also going to call Marcy later in the morning. It was still too early for normal people to be anywhere but at home having breakfast. I sat drinking my coffee trying to work out what I would do. I was convinced that Natasha was a victim and Lucius was a villain. I was desperate to tell her that the file had been changed, and she was being duped but I didn't know how to do it. I was hoping that Marcy's uncle had done some work on the pictures he was sent. I wanted to find outt about Lucius and also about Gina or whatever her name was. Gina had told me Lucius was a toad and a scammer and now I it was evident that she was working with him. I feel like a jerk for believing her crap. Mind you I have no experience with people like Lucius and Gina so I wouldn't know bad if it bit me.

After I finished my coffee I walked back to the office and arrived at the same time Natasha and Lucius arrived. "Hi Siobhan, I hope you had a good evening." "Thanks Natasha, I did actually. I found the file you were looking for and I left it on your desk." I said. "When did you find it?" I looked at Lucius and then back at Natasha, "I found it this morning. I started early and after a few minutes I found it and left it for you." The look on Lucius face was unbelievable. He's probably going to murder me, or put a hit out on me or something even worse, mind you having a hit put out on you is pretty up there in the nasty stuff department. I don't know why I admitted to being in the office early. It was a dumb thing to do but my mouth was possessed by the devil, and I couldn't stop myself.

The combination of working my tail off, walking the beasts, my early rising, and the stress of being a major blabbermouth had made me completely and utterly exhausted by the end of the day. I avoided being alone with Lucius, or taking Gina's phone calls and left the office at exactly five o'clock. Marcy was going to come over after dinner, she said she had some news for me. I took the subway all the way home, and if I wasn't such a cheapo, I would have taken a cab. Dinner was ready when I got home and after eating my weight in spuds and pork chops I went upstairs to lie down. "Mom, could you wake me up in an hour, Marcy is coming over."

"Sure honey but if you're that sleepy shouldn't you just go right to bed," Mom said. "It's okay, I just need a quick nap that's all." If I went to bed after dinner I would be awake and ready to go at two in the morning. My body is a seven-hour sleep kind of machine, it operates at maximum efficiency after seven hours, not eight or six. Sleeping any longer is pretty much impossible for me, and if I do manage a couple of more hours, I have serious dead head and zombie eyes the entire next day.

I had just put my head down, or so it seemed, and Mom was shaking me awake. "Siobhan, Marcy is here. She's in the kitchen having dessert. Splash some water on your face and come down." I did as my Mom suggested and a couple of minutes later I was in the kitchen having a cup of coffee and a cookie with Marcy and Mom. After about twenty minutes of talking Mom said she had some laundry to do and so Marc and I went up to my room to talk.

"You go first, what did your uncle find out?" I said. "Well it appears that there isn't any undercover sting operation going on anywhere that he could find. Gina or whoever she is, is a con artist, his words not mine. He's still checking on her and Lucius. You were right to be suspicious of her. She's working with Lucius but doing 'what' is still not known. The other one Georgette, has a record for writing bad cheques, and was given a warning, nothing too earth shattering. He said Lucius was someone they knew about, but nothing so far on what he's been up to." I sat back and said, "I don't know why I'm not surprised about Gina. She was okay with me but a bit too forward with her information if you know what I mean. If she were really undercover she wouldn't ever have told me about it. She blurted it out pretty quickly. Is your uncle interested in what is going on?" "Well here's the thing, he wants to talk to you about the place. Apparently they've been keeping a watch on Natasha's operation for a while now. Nothing big or serious or anything like that, but they're definitely watching the place. Do you want to get together with him? I think you should, at least for your own protection if nothing else. What was it you were going to tell me anyway?" I told Marcy about what happened with the file, "I decided to return it, pretending like it was buried under a pile of papers and be done with it. I got to the office early because I didn't think I could pull off the, 'look what I found' routine if Natasha was in the office. Anyway, I got there early and noticed that the alarm wasn't set, but never thought anything of it. I put my bag away and walked into Natasha's office and put it on her desk. As I was going back to my desk I heard voices and for some reason I ducked under my desk and hid. A few seconds later I heard Lucius and Gina in the office talking, and the two of them went into Natasha's office. A couple of minutes later they left. I stayed under the desk for quite a while after they left. I swear I nearly peed myself I was so nervous. I went into Natasha's office and saw the file sitting there where I had left it. I opened it up and there was nothing in it but a couple of old memos. Nothing like I saw when you and I went through it. They had taken out all the stuff that would incriminate them." Marcy sat staring at me for a few seconds, "Wow, you must have been scared stiff. What are you going to do?" I told her I was just going to act like nothing was different, but I wanted to talk to her uncle. "Set something up for tomorrow if you can. I think something stinks but I'm not sure what. I know Georgette is a nothing in the whole equation. I think she's just a silly dough head with big ideas." "I think you're right. I'll get in touch with my uncle today and see when he's available. We'll meet at my place. My parents have their bowling night tomorrow so we'll be alone."

We sat and talked for another hour or so. Just as Marcy was getting up to leave I got a call on my cell. It was a call from Gina. I mouthed her name to Marcy before I answered it. After a minute or so I disconnected. "She wants to get together tomorrow night but I told her I was busy and would meet her the next night. I don't know what she wants but she seemed anxious," I said. "You need to be really careful. She could be a hit man or something. You never know," Marcy said. In a matter of an hour or so we had left the realm of snooping and larceny to hit men and danger. She was right though; I was going to be very careful.

After she left I sat with my folks and watched some TV for a while then went up to bed. Even with my nap I felt bushed.

Chapter 20

Thankfully the next day was completely busy and very uneventful. I had a lot of stuff to get ready for the charity event and some basic office housekeeping stuff to do for Natasha. Marcy called toward the end of the day to tell me to meet at her place at seven o'clock. I was actually looking forward to telling her uncle everything that I knew. I wanted to have someone who knew everything on my team, someone besides Marcy that is.

I got home and after eating dinner and changing into some jeans I walked over to Marcy's place. Her uncle was already there, I don't know him really well but I have met him a few times. Marcy made some coffee and the three went into the living room to talk. "Marcy has been telling me about this place you work. You should be very careful, I don't know what's going on there, but I have a feeling it's not exactly kosher. This Gina babe has got me interested. Why would she tell you she was undercover?" "I think she thought I would really dig around for her if I thought she was working for the police. I got suspicious because she told me about being undercover way too quickly. It's not something you would do if you were really a cop, right?" I said. "Well, she certainly isn't a cop. Her real name is Gina Krazinski and she is one tough babe and dangerous to boot. I just don't know what she's doing working there pretending to be an escort. I told my Lieutenant about her and he knew her background. I didn't tell him anything else, not yet anyway. What do you think she's up to?' I told him about the file and her relationship with Lucius and what I heard, "She told me that Lucius was her undercover target. Why would she say that?" I asked. "It's hard to say, she might be testing you to see if you would mention anything to your boss or him. She could also want you to keep tabs on him for her. She doesn't strike me as the trusting kind. Whatever her reason or motive is, it's a dangerous one, I'm positive of that." I told him about Gina's call and about our getting together tomorrow night. "I don't know what she wants to meet me for. I don't have anything to tell her. What should I do?"

The three of us sat tossing around various scenarios for the next ten minutes, "I think you should just listen to what she has to say, and be very careful what you say to her," He said. I told them how I had told Natasha, in front of Lucius, about coming in early and finding the file and putting it on her desk. "I think she wants to find out what you know. Lucius probably told her you were in the office early the morning they took stuff from that file." Marcy said. Her uncle agreed with her and so did I. Why else would she call me?

Marcy's uncle left saying he was going to keep on checking into Lucius and I promised to keep him in the loop. After he left I said, "I feel better knowing that your Uncle Frank knows what's going on. At least he can keep an eye on things and if anything pops he'll be there." Marcy agreed and said, "Uncle Frank is a real straight shooter, he'll be all over this once he knows what's going on, and trust me, he'll figure out what's going on pretty soon." "I'm just worried about Natasha. I know for sure she is innocent and I wish I could give her a heads up. I don't want her to get in trouble or anything like that. That prick Lucius is a snake in the grass and he's out to bury her I just know it."

After another hit of coffee I left to walk home. Ever since this whole Lucius thing kicked into high gear I'm walking a whole lot faster and looking over my shoulder. I am such a drama queen at times.

When I got home my mom was waiting for me, "Siobhan your Aunt Sara called after you left. She and Uncle Pat and Conor are coming over on Saturday. I hope you're around." I gave my best impersonation of excitement and said I'd be around.

Aunt Sara and Uncle Pat aren't really my aunt and uncle, they've just been my parent's friends for years. They were best man and maid of honor at their wedding. Conor is their pimply son. He's about a year and a half older than me and the last time I saw him, about three years ago, he was a royal pain in the ass. Bad skin, bad hair and bad breathe and a totally bad attitude.

With the big visit to look forward to I went to my room and got ready for bed. There was no way around it, I would have to sit with Conor for at least two hours and probably, at Mom's insistence, take him out for a coffee or something. What kind of guy hangs with his parents anyway? Shit you outgrow that by the time you're twelve for crap sake. Oh, boy another swell, action-packed weekend to look forward to. I live such an exciting life that I almost can't stand myself.

Chapter 21

Natasha and I spent the morning going over the next event that and working on the upcoming reception. After the two of us had scarfed down a couple of Mom's meatloaf sandwiches, we got ready to go to Saks. It was a shopping trip for Natasha. She was looking for a few new cocktail outfits and wanted me to help her pick. As if. "I haven't got the best taste in the world. I'm not exactly a fashion plate, in case you haven't noticed." Natasha was laughing and said, "I know you're not a fashion expert but I trust your judgment and the look on your face tells me volumes about how you feel." After she said that I thought hmmm, I really need to work on my poker face. I had no idea I wore my feelings so obviously.

Lucius picked us up outside the brownstone and drove us to Saks. "Don't worry about picking us up Lucius, we'll cab back." I kept my head down and tried hard not to look at him. I didn't want him to be able to read me. It was difficult what I really wanted to do was snarl at him like a friggin' dog.

After an afternoon of shopping we finished with Natasha finding a bunch of outfits that were perfect for her. When we got back to the office, and Natasha joined me as I walked Lola and Coco. We each took one leash. It was actually a nice way to spend time. "Boy, am I glad I'm not doing the stooping and scooping. That would make me gag," Natasha said as she watched Mr. Personality pick up the dogs ass leavings. We both laughed and walked back to the brownstone. After Natasha went back to her office I called Marcy and told her where I was going to meet Gina. "Do you think you should be there just in case? I'm getting a little paranoid and I don't trust Gina one little bit." I said. "I was going to suggest it to you. I'll do it the same as I did before, not the same outfit or anything, but you get my drift." I know I'm a wiener and I joke about Marcy and her flair for drama, but I felt relieved that Marcy was going to have my back. She always would, I know that and it made me feel better.

I didn't go home after work but hung around catching up on some work and then got cleaned up a bit, by cleaned up I mean trying to drag a comb through my crowning 'gory' and slapped a bit of lipstick on checked the pits for deodorant run down, and hit the road.

Gina was waiting for me when I got to the bar. She waved me down and I joined her at the table. "Hey, how are you?" I asked. My voice sounded a bit chirpier than it should have, but I couldn't help it. This was major 'awkward'. Gina looked at me for a couple of beats and then said, "Everything is great. I just thought I'd like to get together with you and see if you have heard or seen anything strange or unusual going on at the brownstone. I haven't heard from you in a while so I thought we could touch base." Oh boy, I had to figure out something to tell her. "Georgette and me have gotten together a couple of times and I'm supposed to meet with her and her partners soon. I think she's pretty harmless if you want my opinion. Other than that nothing seems to be shaking. I don't see much of anything. My job is pretty tame." Shit if only she knew. "Nothing going on with Natasha? Did you see anything strange or hear anything?" she asked. Now I'm feeling like she is putting me on the spot and I'm getting pissed, "See or hear what? I work as a clerical assistant and that's it. I don't know anything about anything. I have no idea what you think I could hear or see. If I did notice anything unusual I would have told you." Gina was a bit taken aback by my answers. "I was just asking that's all. I know you would have told me if you heard or saw something. I guess I'm just getting a bit anxious that's all." After a few more awkward moments we chit chatted away a half-hour and then she stood up to leave. "You'll let me know right away if you hear anything that's even a little strange, right?" Gina said. I told her I absolutely would and then I watched her walk out of the bar. I stood up and looked around for Marcy and noticed her off in the corner in disguise. This time she was wearing a backward baseball cap, a t-shirt, glasses and jeans, oh yeah and she was chewing gum like crazy. What a knucklead. I gave her an eyebrow wiggle, and left the bar. I walked towards the coffee shop and a few minutes later, I watched as Marcy headed in the same direction.

I was sitting in a booth having a cup of coffee and Marcy sat down opposite me. "What do you think of my disguise? Pretty cool right? I think the gum made all the difference, no doubt about it. Anyway what did the bitch want?" "The disguise is great. Once you started chewing the gum I had no clue it was you." Marcy was laughing, "So what did she want?" "I think Lucius told her I was in the office when they pirated the file. She was trying to figure out what I knew and if I heard anything or saw anything. I think she knows I know something, but she didn't come right out and say it. I gave her crap right back though; she started to kind of cross-examine me like I was a criminal or something. It pissed me right off and gave it right back to her."

We finished our coffee and, we walked home together. By the time I got in the house I felt pretty tired and after talking to my parents I went to my room. After getting changed and crawled into bed I fell asleep in a half a second maybe less.

The next morning after I finished my breakfast I said goodbye to my folks and when I stepped outside I saw the limo waiting for me. I stopped in my tracks, I was shit scared, suppose he was going to abduct me, take me somewhere and kill me, or something even worse. The worst possible things that could happen swirled through my mind in a half second and then Natasha popped her head out of the door, whewww. “Hi Siobhan, hop in we’ve got some shopping to do and I want to go to the printer to check on the programs.” I hoped she didn’t notice the look of total relief on my face.

We stopped at a lingerie shop and Natasha picked up a bunch of new knickers and bras. Talk about expensive; my whole wardrobe isn’t worth what she spent on a couple of bras. We stopped by a deli and Lucius went in and picked us up a couple of sandwiches, which we ate in the car. We got back to the office in time for me to give the dogs their afternoon gallop. After they were finished frolicking I headed back to the office with the little darlings. I decided to take a different route and I was rounding the corner on my alternate route and who do I see getting out of the limo, Gina and two seconds later Lucius is at her side and they give each other an overly familiar hug. I pulled the dogs behind me, and trust me it wasn’t easy, and I watched the two of them go into the building. After they went inside I waited a minute or so then walked past the building, taking note of the address. The dogs and I walked faster than usual back to the office. After handing their leashes off to Jenkins I walked to my office. I walked in and as soon as I got to my desk my phone rang. It was Georgette, she wanted to know when we could get together. I told her tomorrow after work would be good for me, so we agreed to meet at the café. After I hung up I went in and told Natasha I was going home and would see her in the morning. “I’m going to be working from home tomorrow. Lucius and I have a lot to go over so if you need me call me on my cell.”

On my way home I was thinking that tomorrow I was going to

do some serious snooping. No one was going to be around to interrupt me, so it would be clear sailing for me.

My folks were out that night so after eating the buffet my mom left warming in the oven I plugged into the TV and clicked my way through three hours of mindless viewing entertainment. I called Marcy and a couple of other buddies and after a thoroughly enjoyable evening of nothingness, I hit the old fartsack. Teehee.

Chapter 22

The next day was great. I got a lot done and managed to finish up all the outstanding work, and by noon I was ready for lunch and then an afternoon of snooping. First thing I did was phone Marcy and give her the address of the place where I spotted Lucius and Gina. "I'll check the tax rolls and see what I can find out. I'll let you know tonight. Are you around?" I told her about meeting Georgette. "I'll call you when I get home. I don't think I'll be out that late. Trust me, after the basic niceties and polite 'how have you beens', it's pretty hard to keep a conversation going with her for more than a half hour."

In order to snoop uninterrupted and fearlessly I decided to lock the door to our offices. I carefully went through Natasha's desk but basically found nothing of interest and after looking around her office I went back to my office and took down some of the accordion type files that I first snooped in. I went through each one pretty thoroughly and then copied the CD in each file. I honestly don't know what I thought I would find but I kept on snooping. After reviewing all of the files and copying everything I could I put everything back where it belonged and dusted the entire office – fingerprints you know. I am such an ass.

By the time I had finished my espionage it was the end of the day. I had a handbag full of CD's and copied paperwork and the guiltiest feeling I had ever had in my life. I felt like a friggin' turncoat and the worst human on earth. The feeling lasted about as long as it took for me to walk over to the café and meet Miss Knucklehead. Of course she was late and kept me waiting a half hour. She sailed into the room and plunked her ass down and said nothing. No sorry I'm late, no how are you, nothing, the ignorant trout. Normally I would have said something, but I didn't say a word and after a few minutes of total silence Georgette put down her cell phone and said, "Is something bothering you. You're very quiet, are you mad at me?" I stared at her for a few seconds and then said, "No, not mad, don't care. What do you want to talk about? Why did you want to meet me?" "I get it you're angry because I was late. You know me I'm always late I can't help myself, it's who I am." I was sure smoke was starting to come out of my ears, "You can't help yourself. What are you some kind of idiot? Of course, you can help yourself; you just don't bother trying. No wonder people don't take you seriously, you don't take yourself seriously. You're rude, self-possessed and you act like a total moron. Snap out of it and start acting like a human being or quit calling me." Georgette sat staring at me then she burst into tears, and like I told you she is some ugly when she cries. "Stop crying for crap sake. Just grow up okay or someone is going to take advantage of you big time," I said. "I know you're right I act like a jerk most of the time. Please don't write me off. I'll try to do better. I called you because my so-called partners gave me these papers to sign and I want you to look at them before I sign them. They don't seem right to me, but I might be more than a little paranoid." She stopped pouting and crying and talked with what appeared to be a certain sense and intelligence. "Georgette, I like you a lot I just don't like the way you act sometimes. I think you could be great if you took more ownership on your life. I'm your friend and I'm on your team,

I've got your back. Give me the papers, and I'll look over them tonight and we can get together tomorrow after work and go over them. Is that okay with you?" Georgette had a big smile on her face, "You're the best, I really appreciate this. I'll call you tomorrow and we can make arrangements. Maybe you can come to my place so we won't be overheard or interrupted." "That's a great idea, call me and let me know what time and all that." After we both finished our drinks we got up and I took the subway home and Georgette flagged down a cab. Therein lies the difference between the two of us.

When I got home I spent a couple of minutes with my folks, then went to my room to call Marcy. I told her about the whole deal with Georgette. "Good for you that you laid it on the line to her. She needs to get a hold of herself. She sounds like a real bubblehead. Anyway, are you going through the paperwork tonight?" I told her I was and then signed off and got to it. Within the first five minutes I realized that they were taking Georgette for a hayride. They wanted her to front the whole organization but she wasn't ever going to benefit financially from being the titular head. They expected her to do exactly what she was doing now and they would be taking their cut and basically she would be doing the same thing she was currently doing with Natasha. The problem was her name was on the deal, and if they were doing any funny business then it was her ass on the line. It was a win win for them and a kick in the head for her. I made some notes on what I had read so far and some suggestions on how to make changes. I felt glad that I was going to help Georgette. She was a jackass, but I could tell she had a heart. Oh hang on a second, I'm getting a little carried away with myself, she might have a heart, but the jury is still out on that point.

Just as I was getting ready for bed my cell rang, it was Georgette, "Siobhan, my partners called and they want me to sign by tomorrow. What should I tell them?" I told her to tell them that she hadn't finished reviewing the paperwork and they would get them back the day after. “Suppose they say no?” I said, “Georgette, trust me they are bullying you, and they need you more than you need them. I will be at your place right after work tomorrow and we can go over everything then. Just tell them you aren’t finished reviewing and that you will be in touch when you are. You are in the driver’s seat not them. Got it?” She was a lot happier after we talked and I was sure she would hang tough. After we hung up I went right to bed. All this espionage and snooping was wearing me down.

Chapter 23

The next day absolutely flew by. I went out at lunch and gave Marcy a call and told her about Georgette being threatened. Marcy told me her uncle had called and she was going to get in touch with him later. “I’ll let you know what he says. What time will you be home?” I told her I would call her when I got home and then I hung up. I found a park bench and sat and thought about all the intrigue I was in the middle of. Usually the only thing I was ever in the middle of with my previous summer jobs were fries and burgers. Look at me now, wearing swishy cocktail dresses, organizing charities and helping the police solve crimes. Wow what a summer.

I worked away till five and then Georgette called to tell me she was home, gave me her address and told me she had something to tell me. I told her I would be there in an hour and hung up. I was wondering what she had to tell me. I hoped she hadn’t signed anything. After clearing up my desk and spending a half hour with Natasha sorting out last minute details for the event tomorrow I left the office.

I got to the address Georgette gave me and rang the bell. She answered in two seconds and I took the elevator up to her apartment. Her place was surprisingly cute and tidy. Who knew? It was a typical one-bedroom type of apartment but Georgette had decorated in a fluffy, girly style, not my style, but very Georgette. "Hi, come in, take a seat and I'll get you some lemonade. Is that okay?" "Perfect, I really like your apartment. It's very you." Georgette came walking back into the room with lemonade and sat down beside me on the sofa. "So what did you have to tell me?" I asked. "It's nothing really except that I stood up to my partners and they backed off like you said they would. It felt really good." "I'm so glad you stood up to them. Some guys are total assholes. Anyway these documents are not good for you. Your name is on the contract as the owner operator, but all you get is what you earn. You don't share any of the profits, and if they do anything illegal it's your ass that's in a sling not theirs. It's the same situation you're in with Natasha only if they go bankrupt or pull a fast one you're the one that's on the hook." Georgette sat staring at me, "I had a feeling that's what it was all about. I feel like such an idiot." Her voice was cracking and I was thinking, 'don't do the ugly crying thing, I couldn't take it', but she managed to control herself. "What should I do? They want a signed deal by tomorrow." I sat for a minute thinking I'm too young to give advice. What the hell am I doing here? "I think, first of all who cares what they want. Secondly you don't need them okay. If you want to start your own escort service do it on your own. You don't need a pile of crooks for partners. Have more faith in yourself. If you really want to run your own business, then just do it." Georgette sat silently listening then she said, "You're right. I don't need those guys. I must be completely stupid to have gotten involved with them in the first place. I'm going to tell them forget it. I'm scared though, suppose they threaten me or something like that?" I thought for a minute then said, "Okay, tell them you'll meet them at lunch tomorrow. Make it the coffee shop that we go to okay. I'll go with you and the two of us will deal with it." Georgette started to cry again, "You'd do that for me?" "Stop crying okay, you're my friend of course I'd do that for you. Now let's call this guy and tell him where to meet us." Georgette stopped crying and called the guy and then after she hung up she said, "He wasn't happy. He doesn't like being dictated to by any woman. What a total asshole."

We talked for another half hour or so and then I got up to leave. "You need to think about what you want to do with your life. Decide what you want and go for it. There's nothing you can't do if you believe in yourself." And with my sermon complete I left Georgette's place promising to meet at the café at noon the next day.

When I got home I had a sandwich, I think Georgette lives on air, and I sat talking with my folks before going up to my room to call Marcy. I told her about Georgette's plight and my solution and she said, "You're great, Siobhan to the rescue. I hope she appreciates what a terrific friend you are, and how much you're helping her. Anyway, Uncle Frank told me that Lucius is some pretty bad news. He said that Natasha and Lucius were an item for a few years, but then she tossed him out because she caught him fiddling more than the books. If you get my drift." I told her I got her drift and asked her, "Why did Natasha take him back? If he's that oily why give him the time of day?" Marcy said that she had asked her uncle the same question but he didn't have an answer. "Maybe she felt sorry for him. She's really nice, and I could see her doing that. I wonder if he is her partner or something? I'm going to go over all those CD's that I copied. Maybe there's an explanation or information on one of them." Marcy agreed and after we talked for a few more minutes we hung up. I told her I'd call her tomorrow after the Georgette thing.

I got out my laptop and put in the first CD. I haven't got a clue what to look for, and I wouldn't know fraud or anything illegal if it bit me my big old flabby ass. I made some notes and after the first CD I was bushed and shut down my computer.

I went back downstairs and sat in the kitchen with my mom. "I'm looking forward to seeing your Aunt Sara and Uncle Pat this Saturday. I hope you and Conor can spend a little bit of private time together." I nodded enthusiastically, "It'll be great to see him again. How's he doing anyway? Is he still in school?" "I think he is dear. Sara said he is doing really well, and he has a lot of prospects lined up for when he finishes. He's studying law you know." I don't know what kind of prospects someone has when they're just starting their law degree but I'm not going to dump a bucket of water on anything my Mom or Aunt Sara says or thinks. "Wow that's great that he has his whole life sorted just like that. Tell me Mom why would a guy his age come out with his folks? Don't you think that's a bit odd?" My Mom was kind of embarrassed and said, "I know honey, it does seem kind of odd. Maybe he just wants to see you, or perhaps he didn't have anything going on that day. I don't know, but I'm just happy to see them all." After talking for a few more minutes I helped Mom clean the kitchen and then went to bed.

I got up early and had a breakfast with my parents. I took my time because I had planned on taking the subway all the way to work. I reminded my Mom that it I had the event to go to that night and wouldn't be home until late.

Chapter 24

Natasha and I worked solidly, even foregoing the morning beast walk. Mr. Stoop and Scoop was on his own with the little darlings. Bye eleven thirty I told Natasha I had to meet Georgette and I would be back by one. I got to the café and Georgette was waiting. We didn't have long to wait, her partners arrived a few minutes after twelve. I could tell by the looks on their faces that they didn't appreciate me being there. Georgette introduced me and we all sat down. "So Georgette, did you review the papers? Lawrence Farber asked. "I did and have decided that I'm not going to sign them. They are not what I expected or wanted. Who do you think you're dealing with? I'm not stupid. I see what you are trying to do, and I think it stinks, so we are done and so is the deal. The three men at the table were looking at me and Georgette like we'd just admitted to murder. "What do you mean you're not interested any longer? You can't back out now. We've rented the space and all that sort of shit. Who do you think you are?" I was listening and realized that he was using a pretty threatening tone. "You heard what she said. She is through with you and your big assed plans. You tried to pull the wool over and she figured it out pretty quickly. Too bad so sad about the rental and all that, you never asked Georgette her opinion so suck it up buster." Lawrence and his buddies sat staring at me like I had two heads. “And furthermore if you bother her or threaten her, we’ll call the police lickety split. Understand? Come on Georgette let’s go.” Georgette handed them the papers they wanted her to sign. She had scribbled all over them with happy faces, swear words and hangmen. The signature page was ripped to pieces. “Bye all.” The two of us race walked out of the café. We ran up the street and ducked into Starbucks. “Go sit and I’ll get us some coffees,” I said. After sitting down the two of us started laughing hysterically. “You were fantastic. You were awesome, the look on their faces was totally unbelievably funny,” Georgette said. “You did pretty darn good yourself girl. We should be damn proud of ourselves. But you have to be very careful, those guys were pretty pissed so don’t take any chances.” She said she would be real careful. “I have to get back to the office but give me a call tomorrow or Sunday and we can talk okay.” The two of us walked out together, and then Georgette gave me a big hug. “Thank you so much for being my friend. I really do appreciate it.”

I had a lump in my throat so I extricated myself from her hug and raced back to the office. I hated to admit it, but I almost liked her as a friend. By the time I got back everything was in full swing. The silent auction items were packed up and sent to the venue, the flowers were already there and all I needed to do was get into my fancy ass dress and get my hair fixed and makeup done. Natasha was getting her hair done so I got into my dress and then sat and waited until they were finished with her. After my hair and makeup was done I put my work clothes in a bag and left them at my desk.

The evening was amazing, and everything turned out perfectly and by the end of the night the event had raised a ton of money. I oversaw the silent auction and let me tell you, those rich folks have no problem paying twice what the item is worth just to win it.

By the time I got home my feet were twice their normal size and my hairdo had taken a walk on the wild side. I washed my face, brushed my teeth and fell into bed.

I got up about eight o'clock and took a shower. My folks were already in the kitchen enjoying our Saturday morning ritual, coffee, biscuits and more coffee. It's the one day of the week when my Mom doesn't build a buffet for breakfast. We sit around with the radio going and the newspaper spread on the kitchen table and we read, talk, listen and eat for about a couple of hours. It's great, we get to catch up on the weeks' events, dish the gossip, and discuss what's going on in the family.

My Mom finished her coffee and biscuits and went to the oven and took out more biscuits and a tray of tarts, a cake and some cookies. "Mom, have you been up all night baking?" "Naw, I just got up a little earlier than a normal Saturday morning. I'm going to put a ham in the oven along with some scalloped spuds, mac and cheese and just before dinner I'll make a big salad. You think that's enough?" My Dad was laughing, "No I think you should do a turkey as well and maybe a roast beef. What do you think Shivvy?" "Yeah Mom are you trying to starve our visitors?" Mom threw a tea towel at my Dad and the brought fresh coffee to the table.

Eventually the Saturday 'sit around the kitchen table' club dispersed and I vacuumed the living room and dusted around. I helped my Mom put out some snacks and then went upstairs to change. I did what I could with my hair and then put on my makeup. I stepped back to take in the full effect, not to bad, could be worse but not bad at all. I switched on my computer and took a look at the next CD. After looking at document after document of stuff I didn't and couldn't understand I switched off my computer. My Mom called me that they were pulling into the driveway so I went downstairs to join the welcoming committee.

Aunt Sara and Uncle Pat hadn't changed one little bit, but Conor, hello, he was a different guy. He was a hunk and a half. He'd grown about ten inches I swear, no pimples, perfect hair and teeth.

The guy was a god for crap sake. I was staring at him and my Mom poked me in the ribs so I'd close my mouth. After the usual hugs and so on they all came in and Mom and I went to the kitchen to get the coffee and tea. Dad was taking bar orders and before long we were all ensconced at the dining room table having a good old catch up session.

After about an hour of family talk, I asked Conor if he wanted to go for a walk. He said sure and I went upstairs, grabbed my bag and touched up my makeup and then we both went out the door. We walked in silence for a few minutes then he said, "What's going on with you? Have you got a summer job?" "Oh yeah, I've got the best job I've ever had, ever. I'm making great money and I love what I'm doing." And then I told him all about it. I don't know why I told him, but I did, and then I told them about the CD's and all that stuff. "Why don't you let me take a look? I don't know everything but it's sort of in my bailiwick of studies, if you know what I mean." I agreed and after we got back to the house I went upstairs and brought down my laptop and the two of us went into the den to look at the stuff.

We looked at the first disk and he was a baffled as me. "I think the first few documents are just documents and nothing more. It would appear that they are correspondence on pretty mundane subjects. If we could find some legal documents I could maybe decipher them." We kept opening various files and documents until we came across something Conor was interested in, "That's what I'm talking about. It looks like a layout of how a new corporation would work. I think this is a suggestion from their lawyer. Let's copy it onto your hard drive." We continued to review the disks and found the list of charities, bank statements on the escort service and a list of people who owed money to Natasha. That's right, Natasha was in the loan shark business, or so it seemed, either that or she was blackmailing a whole lot of people. "I can't believe she would do that. She's not like that at all. Maybe she doesn't have a clue what is going on?

She isn't the one who looks after the books or paperwork. Lucius is the one who looks after that stuff. I know that for sure, because I've seen him carting around files and paperwork more than once." Conor sat staring at the screen, "She is guilty by association. You should try and find a way to confront her about it. If she is caught she could spend some time in the state hotel. What do you think is going on?"

I wasn't sure I had an opinion on what was going on, but I had an inkling, "I think Lucius and his partner in crime Gina, have been siphoning off money for quite a while. The Rhode Island charity is supposed to be a shell company that Natasha uses to distribute money through. According to her it has been dormant for months. I think Lucius and Gina are slowly cleaning out Natasha's coffers, and once that is done she'll be broke and they'll be gone. I also think that the blackmailing is being done so that the victims put more money into her charities, and that makes more money for Lucius and Gina. That's what I think." I had no idea that was what I thought. It all came to me like lightning. Conor was looking at me like I had just burped in his face. "Shit, for someone who isn't too sure what's going on, you developed a pretty detailed idea of what might be going on."

I was laughing, "Blame it on my overactive Irish imagination. Anyway, I don't know what to do. If I talk to Natasha about my suspicions I have to admit snooping around. If I'm wrong she'll fire me and hate me forever." "Copy those files onto a disk for me and let me take them home to look through. In the meantime I'll try and think of someway you can tip your hat without getting in trouble. Let's get together next week after I've gone over this stuff." We went through the rest of the disks quickly and there was no doubt that someone in the organization was blackmailing a lot of clients. There were lists, and amounts of money due and paid, everything a prosecutor would need to charge Natasha. We went back to the living room and after some coffee and dessert, they left to go home. As Conor was leaving we exchanged cell numbers and he promised to call the following week.

"My goodness Conor sure has changed. What a handsome boy, and smart. I did mention he's studying to be a lawyer? You two make a cute couple. Just saying." "Mom, I barely know him. He is nice I'll grant you that, and he has become a lot better looking, but he probably has a dozen babes nipping at his ankles. We're going to talk next week, so we'll see how things go." My Mom had a huge smile on her face. "Oh, Siobhan you'd two would be great together. I just know it. I can tell by looking at you both. Your kids would be incredible looking and very smart." "MOM."

I helped my folks clean up the kitchen and living room and then went up to my room to call Marcy. "You would not believe Conor. I'm telling you it's like he grew a ton, his skin is perfect, hair awesome and teeth sparkling, plus and this is huge, sweet smelling breathe and no B.O. Of course my Mom has us already married off and all that sort of shite, no surprise there." I told her that I had gone through the disks with Conor and arrived at the blackmail theory. "You're right what else could it be? We need to figure out a way of telling Natasha, without really telling her, if you get my drift," Marcy said. I told Marcy about Natasha's event and all that went on, and then I hung up and got ready for bed.

Sunday is a total lay around day at the Murphy's. We wonder around in our housecoats until noon, and then me and my folks go for a long walk, and depending on the weather either stop for ice cream or hot chocolate. It's a great way to end the week and start another. After we got back to the house I went upstairs to check my e-mails and my phone, I leave it at home when we go for our walks. I was expecting to hear from Georgette but so far I had heard nothing. I wasn't concerned but I was a little surprised. I figured she be calling me for sure once a day, but nothing.

Chapter 25

I woke up the next morning and checked my computer for e-mails from Georgette. I also checked my phone, maybe it rang and I didn't hear it. I decided to call her on my way to work. If she was just too 'head up her bum' lazy to call I was going to cut her off forever, but if something happened then I needed to spring into action. What the hell 'spring into action', I sounded like some stupid Disney hero. What a jackass I am.

I rang her number three times on the way to work and nothing, no voice mail, no warning that the phone was out of service, nothing at all. I had a bad feeling about things. Georgette answers her phone. Georgette loves her phone.

There was a reception at the brownstone coming up so it was going to be a busy week. This reception was for new clients and so the tone was to be more conference like and less partyish. Whatever 'less partyish' meant.

Natasha was working away in her office when I got there. I ducked my head in and said hello and then went and made some fresh coffee for her. After putting together the coffee tray I brought it into her office, "Oh thanks Siobhan, sit down and have a cup yourself. Let's go over the reception details for this Friday." I poured us both cups of coffee and then Natasha handed me some paperwork. "Here's the list of girls I want you to call. I'd like them in here on Thursday for a quick meeting. The caterer will be our usual but you decide the kind food we should order. I was thinking something completely different, what do you think?" I was surprised she wanted me to organize and choose the food, but I was excited as well. "How about a 'Malt Shop' theme, or maybe Japanese. Something other than the chi chi stuff that you get everywhere else." Listen to me the 'meatloaf kid', suddenly a canapé expert. "I like the idea of Japanese, I also like the 'Malt Shop' theme but I think that would be good for one of the charity events. As a matter of fact it would be perfect. Juke boxes, drive-in restaurants, french fries, burgers, it would be quite fabulous. I digress, let's go with the Japanese theme." "What about some Japanese lanterns hanging around and some simple Asian floral arrangements?" I said. "Perfect, just not to overly themed, subtle, if you know what I mean." We sat sorting out details for another hour or so and then I went back to my desk. I had my list of girls to call, Georgette being one of them, so I called her number again. No answer, nothing at all. I was definitely getting a little concerned.

I made a few more calls and then took the beasts for their walk. After they were done romping and dumping, I walked them back in the direction where I had spotted Lucius and Gina. As I rounded the corner I spotted Lucius with Georgette's 'sort of' ex-boyfriend and partner Lawrence Farber. Holy crap, what the hell was going on? I was feeling very uneasy and decided to contact Marcy so she could put her uncle on alert. I wanted him to know what was going on and what I had seen. I stood watching the two of them talking and they both went inside the building. I remembered that Marcy was going to check on the building ownership and let me know what the status was.

I got back to the office and after returning the phone calls and giving the girls the information about a Thursday meeting, I called

Marcy. I told her about Georgette being MIA, and spotting Georgette's guy with Lucius in front of the same building I had spotted Gina and Lucius going into. I said, "Do you think you should tell your uncle about all this?" "I'm way ahead of you. I told him after you told me. I couldn't get anywhere with the building ownership search so he's taking a look for us." "What should I do about Georgette? Maybe I'll wait until tomorrow, she's pretty flakey and she may just be at a spa for a couple of days or buried under the sale racks at Bloomies," I said. "I think you're right. Wait until tomorrow and if you don't hear from her, I'll meet you and the two of us will go to her apartment. You remember where it is right?" Marcy said. "Yeah, I know where it is. I hope she's not been kidnapped or murdered or worse." "Shit, what's worse than murder Shiv?" I was laughing at myself. "Nothing I suppose, no hang on a sec, how about 'disemboweled by pirates', that's worse than ordinary murder any day," I said. "Talk to ya later knucklehead," Marcy said as she hung up.

It was my Zumba night so I finished off my to do list and then said goodnight and hopped the subway home. I called Georgette one more time before I left for Zumba class and then again at the restaurant after class. Still no reply.

I got home, checked my e-mails and then sent another one off to Georgette. I didn't want to tip my hat or anything in case her e-mails were screened. I just told her about the Thursday meeting and asked her to be in touch. I had a quick cup of coffee with my folks then went back up to my room and got ready for bed. I'm telling you whomever invented Zumba is a sick SOB, everything hurts, even my ass.

I tried Georgette's number one more time and then hit the hay.

Chapter 26

I got up early so I could have breakfast with my folks. After breakfast I stepped outside and Natasha was standing by the limo smiling. It was a beautiful day and I guess she wanted to soak up some rays. Why else would she be standing outside her car in my neighborhood? “Hi Siobhan, ready for a bit of shopping?” I climbed into the car and she said, “I thought we’d go to Saks and then visit a garden centre to try and find some lanterns and Japanese type plants. What do you think?” “I found a place that will rent props like miniature pagodas, bonsai trees, paper umbrellas, things like that, we could drop into that place.” “Great, let’s do that after Saks.”

We got back to the office by one o’clock and after we unloaded the car I nipped out to get us some lunch. While I was out I tried Georgette again and no answer. I called Marcy and told her and she agreed to meet me outside after work. I was feeling very uneasy and decided to tell Natasha that I had failed to reach Georgette. I wanted to see the look on her face, and see how she would react to the news.

Once I got back to the office the two of us sat at her desk to eat lunch. I had decided to tell Natasha about Georgette. After I finished telling her, she put down her sandwich, “That isn’t like her at all. She always answers her phone it's like an appendage to her. Something is up." "I agree, I have her home address. I will keep on calling the rest of the day and then my friend and I will go over to her place and check to see if maybe she's sick or something," I said. "Good idea. Let me know right away whether you get in touch with her or not."

I finished up my work and continued to call Georgette intermittently for the rest of the day. No dice, no Georgette. I cleaned up my desk and stuck my head in Natasha's office. "I'm on my way over to Georgette's place. I'll call you after," I said. "You be very careful. I don't like the feeling of this. Call me right away and if you have any problems call 911 immediately. Okay?" I nodded and left the room. Marcy was waiting in the lobby for me. "There you are. This place is pretty swishy, of course it has to go some to beat the lobby of the library I work in." The two of us laughed and then left the building. I told Marcy that I had told Natasha about my inability to reach Georgette, "She was genuinely upset and worried. I'm to call her the minute were done skulking around." "Please, it's not skulking it's investigating. Skulkers wear much darker clothing," Marcy said. "You are such an ass. 'Skulkers wear much darker clothing', dickweed."

We got to her apartment and stood waiting until someone let us in. We stood at her door knocking for a few minutes. "No one is answering. Maybe she has a key under the mat or on the door trim," Marcy said as she ran her hand across the door frame producing a key at the end of her swipe. "Voila! The key." "Are you serious she actually left a key up there?" We knocked one more time then stuck the key in the door. We walked into the living room and it looked pretty much the same as it did when I had visited. "I'll check the bedroom," Marcy said and I followed. I felt very nervous, "Nothing in here and no sign of a struggle or fight. Let's finish looking around and then leave. I don't want to get caught breaking and entering that's for sure," I said. "Maybe we should ask her neighbors if they saw anything," Marcy said. "Good idea, let's get out of here." "Wait a minute, let's check her computer for messages," Marcy said. "Okay but let's make it fast I'm crapping myself here. What have you got running through your veins, anyway ice water?" We found Georgette's laptop and after firing it up we found her e-mail file but it was password protected. "No problem, try 'msperfect' or 'abeauty' see if they work." Msperfect worked on the first try. I swear I'm a genius. "Let's see what we have here. So far it looks like she has read all of her messages. She must be accessing them from a different computer. There aren't any messages to indicate where she is or anything like that. At least we know she read her messages." Marcy said. "That's assuming it was her who read them," I said. "You're right, anyone could have read them. We hacked into her e-mails in a half a second. Let's get out of here. Now I'm getting creeped out."

We got out in the hall and after locking up the apartment and returning the key, we went looking for her neighbors. Most of our knocks were unanswered. One older lady who did answer told us that she never sees Georgette and that she, Georgette, is very quiet. Another young guy who answered his door said he hadn't seen the 'good looking babe' in ages, but if I would give him my number he would call if he spotted her. Nice.

We had gotten nowhere and when we stepped outside I gave Natasha a call and told her about our snooping adventures. "Do you have an emergency contact number for Georgette?" I asked. It had just occurred to me that most employers ask for a contact number when you join the company. "I'll check around. I don't know if we do or not. I'm at home right now so we can look for it tomorrow. Good night Siobhan." Marcy and I caught the subway home and we went to her place and she called her uncle to tell him the news. I talked to him for a couple of minutes and he asked me to find out where she was from, what her date of birth was and so on. I said I would check in the morning and get back to Marcy with the information.

When I got home my mom told me that Conor had called. I decided to keep him waiting, I was tired and to be honest didn't feel like talking anymore. I was really nervous about Georgette. I like guys and all that, but to be honest, they take up a lot of air, if you know what I mean. Guys are high maintenance for women. You have to say the right things, act the right way, and wear the right clothes. Sometimes it's great but a lot of the time it's a big pain in the butt. In other words I'll call Conor at my convenience, which means tomorrow while I'm dog walking.

My mom called me downstairs, "So what did he say? What did he want?" "What did who want or say?" "C'mon Siobhan don't be coy. Did you call Conor back yet?" When I told her I would wait until tomorrow she gasped like I had just stabbed her. "Tomorrow, why not now?" I then explained my high maintenance theory to her and as I said goodnight and went up to my room Mom was yelling, "You'll never get married with that attitude. You'll be alone and lonely." I walked to my room smiling. My Mom is such a drama queen.

I changed into my pajamas and realized I was starving so I went down and made a sandwich for myself and brought it up to my room to eat. I switched on my computer and checked for messages, and then surfed around for an hour or so.

Chapter 27

The next day I went straight into Natasha's office to talk about Georgette, "Hi Siobhan, any word from our friend?" I told her I hadn't heard anything and that I was really worried, "So am I. The fact that her e-mails were all opened and read is a bit worrisome. It could be a good thing or a bad thing. I'm going to look around for some personal information on Georgette. You could look through your office files and see if there is any information anywhere around."

For the next twenty minutes the two of us went through every computer file, paper file and directory we could find, but nothing personal on Georgette showed up.

"What'll we do now? I think we should call the police. Doesn't Georgette have any girlfriends? Maybe I should have checked her computer for contacts. Shit I'm so stupid."

I said, "Never mind Siobhan, before we call the police let's go back to her apartment, just you and me and have another look around. You can check out the computer and I'll go through her things. Don't worry about being caught, I'm an old lady no one would ever accuse me of anything untoward. I'll tell anyone who catches us that I'm her aunt."

We finished off work and then I called a cab and we headed to

Georgette's place. I was pretty relieved that Natasha hadn't asked Lucius to drive us. Anyway we got to her place, got let inside and I knocked several times on her door before using the 'hidden' key.

"You go through her computer and I'll go through her bedroom and check if anything is missing like her makeup and her hair dryer. Georgette wouldn't go anywhere without her beauty essentials. I know that for sure." I logged into her e-mail and found her contact list. It was pretty short but I copied it all onto a flash drive. I then went through her correspondence file but found nothing of importance. I shut down the computer and went to find Natasha. "Anything?" Natasha asked. I waved the flash drive and put it back in my pocket. "You know what? I haven't seen her phone around anywhere. So that's a good thing. What did you find?" I said. "Well, her makeup bag and hair dryer are gone as well as her manicure set, and it looks like half her underwear drawer has gone missing. It appears that our little friend took off on her own," Natasha said. "You're right. What an ignorant bitch. Here we are worrying our heads off, concerned for her safety and all that crap and she's probably at some fat farm burning off a couple of dozen chocolate chip cookies. If that is the case she has lost her one and only friend."

After we had finished looking around her apartment the two of us left, locking the door and returning the key to its 'hiding' place. Once outside I said, "So you think we should just sit tight and wait to hear from her?" "I think so, it doesn't appear that she left under duress or anything like that. I would just forget it for now. She might call later to explain her absence, or maybe not. Either way we've done what we can to get in touch with her." I nodded in agreement and the two of us got a cab back to the office.

I took the dogs out and while I was waiting for them to finish their workout I gave Conor a call. "Sorry I didn't get back to you last night I was kind of tied up. How are you doing? Did you get a chance to look through the files you took?" I asked. He said he had and had discovered some very interesting things in the files. We made arrangements to get together tomorrow night at the café. I hung up and went and got the dogs and walked back to the office grinning like a jerk.

I had a sandwich at my desk and worked right through until five-thirty. I was bushed, and even though I was beginning to be more than a little pissed with Georgette, I tried her number a couple of more times before I left for home.

Gina called me just as I was leaving the office and I decided to ignore her call. I wanted to find out more about her before I spoke with her again. I was hoping that Marcy had found out about the building I saw her and Lucius enter the week before. I didn't have anything I wanted to talk to her about. I had a feeling she was going to ask me about Georgette, and after seeing her with Georgette's former partner, I felt she would probably be on some sort of a fishing expedition.

Chapter 28

When I got in my Mom was home from work and up to her eyeballs in her annual canning program. It's something her and my Dad love to do and make a big deal of it every year. Half the stuff they make they give away, but I think it's the idea of 'making your own' that makes it so special for them. They were starting with peaches and plums and the kitchen was full of baskets and bags of the fruit. The two of them make a schedule every year and post it on the fridge. It's a two-week job and for those two weeks the kitchen is almost out of commission for real food. The most Mom manages is chopped egg sandwiches, cold cuts and pizza, which is fine by me. It's nice to take a break from my Mom's version of a well-balanced diet.

After a dinner of potato chips and pizza I plunked myself down in front of the TV for a couple of hours. Marcy called me on my parent's landline and I told her I'd call her on my cell. I went up to my room and called her back. "I found out through Uncle Frank, that the building is owned by, are you ready for this, 'Rhode Island Commemorative'. It's listed as a place of business and it is being renovated and decorated apparently. What do you think of them apples," Marcy asked. "Wow, that is so blatantly in your face. I bet Natasha has no idea about the place. I know exactly what they're doing now. I have to tell Natasha, at least find a way of her discovering what is going on." I told her about going back to Georgette's place and the fact that all of her basic beauty things were missing. "Natasha is right. A girl like Georgette would never leave without her makeup, hair blower and all her other beauty crap. She is just way to vain to do that. She'll be in touch and I hope she has a real good reason for not contacting you. After all you've done for her. What a bitch!" I agreed and the two of us talked about how to I should get Natasha to discover what is going on. I'm also worried about the blackmailing I know Lucius is up to his eyeballs in. Natasha isn't naïve, and she certainly realizes that her service and her clients' use of the service wields a little pressure on them to help her financially with her charities. But blackmail, she would be completely mortified, totally embarrassed and probably want to shut up shop. After I hung up I sat in bed working out what I would or should do about what is going on. I wanted to help Natasha. If the police get involved she could find herself in a lot of hot water. Her name is all over everything. If they interviewed her clients they would probably say they believed she was behind the whole thing. The fact that all of the accounting and paper work is in her office is also pretty damning. I was wondering if Conor had anything to show me that I hadn't already figured out. One thing was for sure, I needed to do something to help Natasha I just had no clue how to do that.

I fell asleep and dreamt about that dough-head Georgette. She was calling out to me, asking for help. I woke up completely unrested. Disoriented, and I had a massively serious case of deadhead.

I got to work and after two giant lattes, I got the cobwebs blown out of my head and managed to get the boardroom organized for the girls coming in later for a meeting.

I took the dogs out at ten o'clock and while I was out Georgette finally called me back. "Where the hell have you been? I've been worried sick. I thought your former partners had kidnapped you or killed you or something." "Oh, please don't be mad with me. After we left those guys I went home and I locked everything up and then the phone calls started. At first they were just heavy breathing on the other end, then the threats started. They were going to throw acid in my face, break my legs you name it. I didn't know what to do and I didn't want to involve you. It would put you in jeopardy so after a night and the whole of the next day filled with threats, I packed up some stuff and went to spend time with my Gran in Connecticut, and I'm still here, I just didn't call because I thought maybe they could find out through you where I was. I figured they would beat you up for the information." I was so relieved I nearly cried. "Georgette, can you stay put at your Grans'? If you can, do so. I'm trying to sort some things out and I think you're better off there until all this crap is sorted." "No problem, I get along with my grandmother like a house on fire. We're just hanging out and chatting so I can stay here indefinitely. I'll call you in a couple of days and you can let me know how things are going. Is that okay with you?" "Absolutely, I'll wait for you call okay?" I said. "Thanks Siobhan, you're a great friend. No one has ever worried about me before except Gran. I really appreciate you. Thanks." Just as I was about to tell her to think nothing of it, she had hung up.

The call made me feel a whole lot better but I didn't tell Natasha. Not that I didn't trust her but it would mean I would have to fill her in on a lot of stuff I hadn't told her about. Also she might let it slip to Lucius, and he could let the rest of the gang know, and then Georgette would never be safe. I still didn't know how everything fit together but I was pretty sure it did.

I got back to the office and set up the boardroom for the meeting. I wheeled in the newest gowns, set out soft drinks, water and coffee and then left the boardroom.

We had found some great props at the supplier I had tracked down for the reception so I went out into the reception room to work out where everything should go. I didn't want to overdo the look, so I edited a lot of the stuff. If I didn't the party guys will hang everything and the room will end up looking like a badly decorated Chinese restaurant.

I brought lunch for Natasha and me and we ate it at her desk. Chopped egg and pickle on homemade whole wheat bread, coconut squares and carrot sticks. "I swear Siobhan, your Mom has the magic touch with food. She does something to even the most basic food to make it taste delicious. Thank her for the lunches she so kindly makes for us. I have something for her, I hope she doesn't mind." Natasha left her office and came back with a mega gift basket filled with the most incredible skin care stuff, bath products and a big fluffy bathrobe. "Oh my gosh, my Mom loves stuff like that. She'll freak out. You know you didn't have to do that." Natasha smiled, "I wanted her to know how much I appreciate her efforts. I hope she likes it." "Trust me you just guaranteed a life time subscription to my Mom's meatloaf sandwiches."

After lunch I cleaned up, and then waited in the lobby for the girls to arrive. I showed them all into the boardroom and they poured over the dresses for a few minutes before Natasha walked in. "Thanks for coming girls. I just wanted to go over a few things before our Friday reception. We've got a lot of new, potential clients coming to our soiree so we need to be on our best behavior. You need to be classy, well spoken, and do not drink too much. We are having a Japanese sort of theme so it should turn out to be a really great evening." Some of the new girls were looking at Natasha like she was an alien. I'm pretty sure they had no idea what 'classy, well spoken' meant. Some of the newer ones had trouble concentrating on anything that was said, with a rack of designer gowns in the room. Anyway at the end of the talk and the Q & A the girls went back to the rack and the strip down, try on, began. Clearly modesty is a learned thing.

After the girls left Natasha and I walked back to the office. Do you think they got what I was saying? They looked a bit blank. What do you think?" "It's hard to say. They were most distracted by the rack of dresses in the room. The ''shiny object' syndrome I think. We'll see what happens tomorrow night." Natasha laughed her way into her office. "You're a real character Siobhan. A one of a kind."

I went to my desk to finish off some stuff. I was going to meet Conor right after work so I had to spend some time sprucing myself up before I met him. I tweaked my hair, tweaked, who am I kidding my mop is untweakable. I wrestled with my hair, slapped on a bunch of lipstick, some blush and mascara. I wasn't sure if I had overdone the makeup so I went and asked Natasha. I knocked and walked in, "What do you think? Too much war paint?" Natasha chuckled and said, "You look great. Have you got a big date or something?" "Naw, just an old friend who looks like he was photo-shopped. I'm going to put the basket in a big bag to take home with me. Is that alright?" I left Natasha laughing, put the basket in a big garbage bag and walked to the café.

When I arrived his hotness was already seated and waiting for me. He stood up when I got to the table and gave me a kiss on the cheek. "Are you hungry?" he asked. I told him that iced tea would be fine for me. Meanwhile I could have murdered anything on the menu. After a little small talk Conor opened a notebook and started to tell me what he had found out. Basically it was what I had already found out, but I didn't want to say anything. He had clearly done a lot of work on it. I nodded and made some comments. After he had finished I said, "You know what? I think you've hit the nail on the head. Natasha is in trouble. They're draining her bank accounts and moving everything over to the new company. I'm pretty sure they are blackmailing some of the more high profile clients and this Gina character and a couple of the other gals are coming onto these guys and getting the goods on them. It looks bad for Natasha. I need to find a way of warning her but I can't think of a way of doing that without admitting what I've been doing. I'll bet once they've bled her dry Lucius will get her to sign papers giving the whole shooting match to him or some other corporation. He'll probably convince her it's good for her tax bracket or some crap like that. What do you think?" Conor nodded, "I think that is exactly what they plan on doing. We have to stop her from doing anything like that and you're right you need to figure out a way of telling her what you know. Somehow finding a way of letting her discover it on her own. What about this building that is in the Rhode Island Charity thingee. Is there a way to leak those deed or lease papers to her? If she saw them I'm pretty sure she would start to put two and two together. What do you think?" I thought about it for a few seconds, "I think that's a great idea. I just don't know how to do that. How would I get a copy of the papers for the building?" "Let me think about that for a couple of days. There has to be a way. It should be public domain. Maybe I can track down copies and then we can mail it to her anonymously. What about that?" I sat and thought about it. "I think that would work. I would hope that she would follow the trail once she got it in the mail. So far it's the best idea. I haven't got a better one that's for sure. So you can get that stuff?" I said. "No problem just give me a few days and I'll give you a call, and we can sort it out. In the meantime how about going to a ballgame with me this Saturday. I got a couple of comp tickets and I thought you might like to come with me." I was taken aback a bit. He was asking me out on a date, sort of. If you can call a couple of free seats at a baseball game a date. "Yeah, that sounds like fun."

We sat and talked for quite a while and then he walked me to the subway. I was kind of worried he would try and kiss me. Thank god he just gave me a peck on the cheek. "I'll see you Saturday and let you know what the status is." I waved goodbye and went down to the subway platform. I was starving, and could hardly wait to get home and have a bite to eat. Sitting on the train there was a couple of boys throwing an apple back and forth, I nearly jumped in and grabbed the friggin' thing. I don't even like apples that much, but I so hungry I would have inhaled it anyway. Good job my stop was coming up.

When I got home my parents were busy pickling or canning or whatever you call it. "There's a pizza in the oven for you." Mom said. After I got a plate I sat at the kitchen table and chowed down. "I was having an ice tea with Conor, that's why I'm late." My Mom turned around with the biggest smile on her face. "Oh, honey I knew you'd connect with him. He's such a nice boy." Even my Dad was grinning. "Oh for god sake it was just a drink. No biggie. We're still pretty young you know. I'm not looking for a husband or a boyfriend for that matter. He's a nice guy let's just see how things go. I'm going to the ballgame on Saturday with him. He got a couple of comp tickets. It's not a date or anything like that it's just a ballgame so don't go getting all excited." "Okay dear, but he is a nice boy from a good family. You never know okay, you never know, that's all I'm saying." I finished my dinner and remember the garbage bag that I lugged from work. "I nearly forgot Mom, Natasha bought you something." I handed the bag to her, the hand off wasn't very impressive, but that was good because when Mom opened it up she nearly freaked out. "Holy smokes, she bought this for me. Why? This is incredible I love all this stuff. Look at this robe." Mom was tearing through the basket full of stuff, clearly thrilled and delighted with everything." "She wanted to thank you for all the lunches you made for us." "Wow, she didn't have to thank me. I'm happy to do it." Mom said as she tried on her new robe. "I told her that, but she insisted that she wanted to show her gratitude." "Well I'm going to send her a thank you card. Is that okay?" I smiled, "Of course Mom, Natasha would really like that."

Mom and I went through the entire basket and there was everything but the kitchen sink in there. After we finished demolishing the basket I made coffee for us, and after cleaning the kitchen we all sat in the living room and watched some TV.

Chapter 29

I got up early and washed my hair and didn't bother doing any styling, like I ever really do, until I got to work. The hairdresser was going to work his magic later in the day so I just stuck it up in a ponytail.

As usual the place was crazy with activity. I spent most of the morning in the reception room. We were going to have a couple of Sushi chefs prepare the Sushi fresh so I needed to make sure everything was set up properly. The lanterns were strung up and the plants and flowers were arranged around the room. The servers were in costume. I was concerned that the costume thing was a bit over the top but they looked good.

I walked the dogs and when I got back my office was full of girls and dresses. It took about three hours of chaos until the room was empty. Natasha was getting ready so I asked one of the hairdressers if he could do my hair. Of course he could, he was getting paid to do hair, I swear sometimes I'm so nice I could toss. "Hi, do you think you could do my hair?" What a suck I am. Anyway, he finished my hair, and then the makeup guy, who is a lot of fun called me over, "Come to my lair my beauty, I have things to do to you!" I sat in the makeup chair and watched him work his magic. "I wish I could do my makeup the way you do it. You always make me look so glamorous," I said. "It's easy, you have a great face and great bone structure. Just pick the colors I pick and don't try covering you freckles. They're your trademark, own them." I never thought of my freckles as my trademark that's for sure. Maybe he was right I shouldn't sweat them, they are what they are even if they are multiplying at lightning speed.

By the time my hair and makeup were done and I had put on my cocktail dress, squirted a bit of cologne around, and I was ready for the big event.

The guests arrived at almost the same time so the lobby was pretty wild, jammed with people, for a little while. Eventually we got everyone into the reception room and the party got started. About an hour into it Gina walked in. I didn't expect her and to be honest I was pretty nervous. I hadn't returned her calls and basically I was ignoring her. Do you blame me? She's pretty scary. She brought a couple of girls with her that I had never seen before, and they immediately moved out into the crowd. What was she playing at? I went to find Natasha. I spotted her in conversation with the caterer, "Natasha, could I have a word?" I said. "One second dear." I stood off to the side and waited until she joined me, "What's wrong? You look a little upset. What happened?" I told her about Gina and her posse. "Where are they? Show me, let's go." I led Natasha back into the reception room and within a few minutes she had rounded up the women and Gina and had then in her boardroom. "What do you think you're playing at Gina? This is a private party. You can't just round up anyone you spot on the street and drag them along." One of the girls, Tracey, took offence to the 'on the street' comment. "Hey what are you saying. I not from the street, I'm from Brooklyn." I was standing off to the side as the rest of the girls, there were four plus Gina, grumbled and gestured. "Sorry Nats, these gals are buddies and I thought it would be kind of fun to spice up the night with some new blood. No harm, no fowl." She turned to the girls, "C'mon guys let's get out of here." As she and her gang marched out of the room Gina walked up close to me and mouthed the word, "Later". I stood paralyzed thinking, "Did she just threaten me? Should I be worried or scared?" Never mind 'should I be scared?', yes, I was scared.

I walked over to where Natasha was standing and said, "We'd better get back. What was Gina playing at anyway?" I asked. "I'm not sure, but I'm going to find out. Georgette wasn't the one to worry about, it's been Gina all along." The two of us walked back to the reception and with the exception of a couple of drunk newbie girls, and an overzealous old geezer things went well. The room was empty by ten o'clock and I trudged back to my office, retrieved my bag, and then hopped into the cab Natasha had ordered for me.

I called Marcy on the way home and told her about my run in with Gina. "Do you think it was a threat?" I was beginning to think I had overreacted to the 'later' comment. "Oh yeah, that was a threat. I'm talking to my Uncle Frank tomorrow. I want to hear what he has to say. Can you meet me?" I told her about my supposed date with Conor. "Doesn't sound like much of a date to me. Free tickets to a ballgame, whoopee shit. Well, call me when you get home, maybe we can get together after you big date. The ballgame is usually over by five."

I got in the house and my parents were waiting up for me, "You look wonderful. Your makeup looks like you aren't even wearing any. How was the evening?" Mom asked. I sat down on the chair opposite and took off my shoes and rubbed my feet, "It was great. Lots of people showed up and the food was a hit. Sushi, who knew?" "Sushi, raw fish right? What's the big attraction with uncooked food? I don't get it, I've tried it, but it tastes dull to me. The last time me and the gals from the office went to dinner they all wanted to try some Japanese place. I tell you I tried the stuff but it made me gag." I tended to agree with my Mother. I wasn't a Sushi fan, although I didn't mind California rolls or whatever they're called. I went up to my room to change and wash my face then joined them back in the living room. "I'll make us some tea. Do you want a cup Siobhan?" Mom asked. I said I did and my Dad and I sat watching TV until Mom returned with tea and cake. I sat enjoying my parents company for a while then said goodnight and went up to bed.

I had a terrible night, thrashing around, and tying myself up in the sheets until I finally fell asleep. Saturday morning being our lay around time I got up, took a shower, donned my housecoat and joined my parents in the kitchen. After a couple of cups of coffee I started to feel human again. Conor called about an hour later, "I'll meet you in front of the stadium at one o'clock." Before I could answer he had hung up. I was beginning to find him a bit of an ass, but I wanted to stay on his good side until he dug up the papers on that building. I didn't want to show my pissed offedness to my parents, so I plastered a dumb grin on my face and continued drinking my coffee and eating breakfast.

After a couple of hours I went upstairs to get ready. After I was dressed and my hair and makeup done I went to say goodbye to my folks, "Isn't he picking you up?" Dad asked. "No I'm meeting him in front of the stadium." "What kind of date is that? Why can't he pick you up?" Mom said. "I don't know, maybe he's busy and doesn't have time to swing by the house. I don't think he's got a car, so it would be a little inconvenient. Besides, it isn't really a date. It's just a 'let's go to the ballgame' get together that's all." Before the debate expanded into righteous indignation and anger at Conor, I slipped out of the house, yelling 'I won't be late' as I closed the door. I don't know if any guy could measure up to their standards. He'd have to be pretty perfect in every way. Conor isn't there yet, and probably never will be because he failed to pick me up for our 'sort of' date.

I got to the stadium in plenty of time and spotted my 'date' off in the distance. He was chatting away to some guy. I walked up to them and Conor introduced me to his 'friend' Mike. "Mike is going to join us to watch the game. He has a seat a couple of rows up from us. I know you're not a huge baseball fan so can he switch with you? You can take his seat and that way Mike and me can sit together and talk baseball. I hope that's okay. Here's ten dollars for snacks and stuff." I was standing with my mouth wide opened. What the hell kind of guy was he? Ten bucks for snacks, like I'm some five year old getting my weekly allowance. After he said that Mike handed me his ticket and Jackwagon Conor, handed me ten bucks. I was so dumbstruck I followed both of them into the stadium and after we found our seats, and the game began I started to seethe with temper. Never in my life had I been treated so pathetically. The longer I sat, the angrier I got. I was staring at Conor and Mike who were just in front of me and I noticed that the two of them were displaying a friendlier than normal vibe. I got up out of my seat and walked down to where Conor was sitting. "Could I talk to you for a moment," I said then walked up to the exit with Conor in tow. Once outside I said, "Look, I refuse to be treated like that. I am totally pissed with you right now. How dare you invite me here, and then shuffle me off so you can sit with your buddy and talk baseball. You even handed me ten bucks. You are a first class asshole." Conor was standing in front of me with his head hung down. "I'm sorry Siobhan I didn't mean to mislead you. Mike is my boyfriend, not just a buddy. I'm gay and I don't often get a chance to spend time with him. I hoped you would understand, my parents watch me like a hawk. I think they suspect something is up. I don't know what they think they can do about my gayness. I guess they're hoping I'll be cured. I went with them over to your parents place because they insisted I spend time with you. I didn't mean to hurt your feelings, I really like you." He had tears in his eyes and I felt like a first class bitch. "Look it, you should have been straight, bad choice of words, with me. I get it okay, I like you as well but I can tell you one thing for sure I hate baseball. You go back to your friend Mike and I'll head off to meet my friend Marcy." Conor had a look of relief on his face, "Don't worry your secret is safe with me. I think you should be honest with your parents, but that's your call. Are you still looking for the paperwork we talked about?" "Absolutely, I hope to have tracked it down by Monday. I'll call you tomorrow. Thanks Siobhan, you're a real pal." "Anytime Conor. Bye for now."

After he went back to his seat I called Marcy. "Hey I thought you were at the ballgame with Mr. Hunkitis?" "I am at the ballgame, but I'm leaving now. Are you going to be home?" "Yeah, I'm home all day. What's going on?" "I'll tell you when I get there. See you in about a half hour."

When I got to Marcy's place she answered the door before my knock. "Come on in. What's going on?" I gave her a look that was a 'let's go to your room and I'll tell you look', if a look like that exists. If one does I doubt if I could duplicate it. Marcy go the gist and we went to her room. "What the hell happened?" So I told her the entire story. "You've got to be kidding me. He was using you as a piece of bait. What a prick. Why the hell doesn't he tell his folks and get it over with? It's the 21st century for shit sake." "I know, I agree. I actually felt really sorry for him. He was nearly in tears when we were talking. I'm not sure his folks would get it, they're not real progressive, if you get my meaning. I know he really cares about them and he doesn't want them hurt by telling them he's gay. Now I've got to try and figure out what to tell my parents. Mind you they were not happy when he didn't come to pick me up so maybe they've cooled on him a bit." "Your folks would understand about Conor being gay, why not just tell them?" Marcy asked. "Normally I would, but my parents are really close friends of Conor's parents and I'm afraid if my Mom knew, she might blurt something out or let something slip. If that happened they'd both be devastated. I asked Conor if he'd still do the document search for me and he said he would. I have a feeling I'm going to be his 'date' quite a bit over the next while." "So the plan is he will get copies of the title for the building and what? Mail it anonymously or something to Natasha?" "That's the plan. He's going to call me tomorrow and let me know what the status is. I have to tell you what happened last night at the reception. You will not believe it." I proceeded tell Marcy about the uninvited guests and how Natasha dealt with them. "Seriously, they crashed the reception." Marcy asked. "Well they didn't actually crash it because Gina was invited, but technically the rest of them arrived uninvited. I haven't told you the rest. As they were leaving the room Gina got right up in my face and mouthed the word 'later', and she didn't have a happy smiley look on her face." I said. "She threatened you, no doubt about it. That bitch was trying to intimidate you," Marcy said. "It worked, I'm totally intimidated and scared shitless and witless. I think we should meet with your uncle so I can tell him what's going on. What do you think?" "I was going to tell you. My uncle wants to get together as soon as possible, let's see if we can get a hold of him today."

Marcy called and no answer so she left a message for him to call as soon a she can. "Let's go and get something to eat. I'm starved, my treat." Marcy got cleaned up and we went to Anna's Grill. It's a neighborhood kind of place my friends and me have been hanging around for years. There's nobody named Anna that works there nor is there an Anna who ever owned the place. No one has a clue where the name came from. The owners Iris and Manny Bunker bought it name included about fifteen years ago. They haven't ever changed a thing, including the menu and to a certain extent the prices. That's why we hang out there. The prices are great and the food is so so, but there's lots of it. They serve the same gravy with everything. Chicken, turkey, beef, and pork are all coated with the same brown gelatinous liquid referred to as 'Anna's Yum Num Sauce', I kid you not 'Yum Num'. You can opt out of the sauce if you so desire and enjoy a totally unadulterated pork chop or steakette, but be prepared to load on the salt. You have to work pretty damn hard to find a distinctive taste in any of their food. It doesn't stop us from going though, we're loyal customers to the core. We'll probably stop making Anna's our regular once we develop taste buds.

When we got to the restaurant we spotted a bunch of our friends. We all got a bigger booth together, and had a total laugh. Our table was weighed down with fries, onion rings, half eaten sandwiches and burgers by the end of two hours. Most of my friends were like Marcy and me; ordinary type people that have a massive sense of humour and are a load of fun to hang with. I told them all about my great job, it was a job I know anyone of them would love to have. Of course, I didn't go into any detail about the problems or the people." The school year was looming, so we all talked about the course list and stuff like that. Eventually we all left the restaurant. Marcy and I walked back to her place and by then it was a decent time for me to go home.

My folks were waiting for me when I got home. I walked into the kitchen as my Mom put down a cup for me to have some coffee. "So, how was it? Did he behave? Did he treat you with respect?" my Dad asked. "No worries, Conor is a decent guy and knows how to act like a gentleman. We had a good time." I had checked the internet to find out who won the game, just in case I was asked, which I wasn't. "Are you hungry? I've got some left over chicken if you'd like a sandwich." Mom asked. "No it's okay I ate at the ballpark. I'm not hungry at all." "That's nothing but junk food. You need some real food I'll make you a sandwich, eat what you feel like eating." And I wonder why I have a shelf for an ass.

After trying to eat part of the sandwich, which by the way is the size of a baby grand, I went and flopped in front of the TV, and within minutes I was sawing wood. Volumes of food lodged in your stomach will do that to you. My Mom shook me awake a little while later and I dragged my butt up to my bed. Boy I was bushed.

I fell instantly to sleep but woke up at the crack of dawn. It's my nightly limit thing, only so many hours of sleep a night, and if I fall asleep on the sofa it gets factored in to my sleep quota.

I went down to the kitchen and had some coffee. Just as I sat down Marcy called and told me her uncle could see her and me that day. We agreed to meet at the coffee shop at three o'clock. After we all got changed my folks and I went of our Sunday walk, ending at the local ice-cream place for soda's.

We got back, just in time for me to answer my calls and check for e-mails. After I had done that I cleaned up a bit and left to meet Marcy and her Uncle Frank. The two of them were waiting for me at the café. After ordering I said, "Has Marcy told you anything that has happened?" "She told me a bit. I knew about that Georgette girl who went missing but nothing else. From my end I found out there's no one in the force or undercover. That Gina character is a con artist and not to be messed with, so watch yourself with her. My boss is looking into the operation, discreetly, but he wants us to keep an eye." I filled him in on everything that had transpired. I stressed to him that if there was blackmail involved Natasha was innocent. "We'll see what turns up. One thing is for sure if they are blackmailing some of their clients, the victims would believe that Natasha was involved." I told him about the building ownership and our plan to get Natasha to look deeper into her situation, sort of like an alert. "She believes that the Rhode Island Company is just a shell corporation that she isn't using. The building has the Rhode Island Company listed as its owner," I said. "It's a good plan, and it will keep you at arm's length, which is a good thing. Have your friend send a copy to me or you if you don't mind, okay?" "I'll let him know tonight." "Do you think you can get copies of some of the files so I can check them out? It might be tricky but if you can that would be a big help. It may tell us some of the clients they're going after." Uncle Frank asked. "I already have copies of the files. I did it a while ago. I can get you copies of the disks by next week." I said. "That's great. I would just like to review them, nothing will happen until we know if something is going on that we can actually see." "What do you think they are planning to do?" I asked. "My take is that they plan on draining her company dry and move everything over to a new company that they would own and operate. The files will show us how they are doing it. This Lucius guy has her ear so she probably has him looking out for and taking care of a lot of the banking and business side of things. Natasha is in a bad situation and unless she knows to watch her back, she'll find herself losing everything."

I was feeling sick to my stomach. Poor Natasha, I had to help her no matter what I had to do. Of course, if getting killed or having my life threatened was what I had to do, whole different story. I'm not a coward but I'm young and this life threatening business is not what I ever included as part of my growing up plan. Dating, clothes, college, my own car, my own apartment, that the sort of growing up plan I envisioned for myself.

After a few more minutes Uncle Frank had to leave. "Listen, take my advice and be very careful, better still, quit and find yourself another job. These people are dangerous and you could get yourself caught in the middle of a bunch of bad news. Watch yourself Siobhan."

After he left the two of us sat around talking about everything but Natasha and her problems. We finished our drinks and then we both went home. I was feeling worn out. It had been an action packed couple of weeks that's for sure. I got home and after saying hello to Mom and Dad I went up to my room. I switched on my computer and went through my e-mails, sent a few out and then logged on to my school's website. I wanted to see if they had posted my book list yet.

I was about to go downstairs and Conor called me, "Hi there, how was the rest of your day?" I asked. He said it was good and he apologized again and I said that we should just put it behind us. "I'm going to hopefully have the stuff for you by the middle of the week. I'll let you know the minute I put it in the mail," he said. "Could you make a copy for me as well. I told Marcy, my friend, and her uncle who's a cop all about it. He said they were watching the company. When I told him our plan to get Natasha's attention, he thought it was a good one, so thanks so much for your help, I appreciate it." I said. "No problem, we can still be pals can't we? I really like you." "Absolutely, thanks again Conor. I'll talk to you soon." I hung up and sat thinking, 'I'm a freaking magnet for nutbars, Georgette the world's biggest flake, and Conor, Mr. Scaredy Pants whose afraid to admit he's gay, and has absolutely no manners whatsoever and Gina the thug. Defintely a crackpot magnet no doubt about it.

I went downstairs to help Mom with dinner, my Dad was out picking up my Grandmother who would be joining us. Hot damn a meal with the Grandmeister. We were having Italian food for dinner and I set the table so I was out of range of my Grandmother. "Why are you making spaghetti for dinner? You know the trouble Gran has with the long noodles. The table will look like a murder scene by the time dinner is over." Mom started to laugh, "I don't know why. I should know better, but I know she likes pasta. I think the devil made me do it." I was laughing as I finished setting the table. A few minutes later Dad came in with Gran. She had brought some dessert, two apple pies, well her idea of apple pie anyway. "Why two pies Gran? We'll never be able to eat all that pie." She had put the pies on the kitchen table, "There's an apple and lemon pie and another apple and lemon pie. I had to make mix the lemon and the apple together because I didn't have enough apple or lemon to make two pies." I was about to question the logic of two mixed pies, and ask the question 'why not one of each?' but Mom shot me a look so I just went along. Mom said, "What kind of crust is that Mom?" "I was making bran muffins and decided instead of making muffins I would add more bran and make a piecrust out of the mixture. It's better for you." Who could possibly argue with that kind of culinary logic. Nothing in the world like a bran muffin pie crust filled with apple and lemon to keep you regular, and satisfy your love of dessert.

I had to leave the room after that. The look on my Mom's face was priceless. Dinner was going to be hysterical. An hour later we were all sitting around the dining room table. Gran was wrestling with her spaghetti like it was alive and in attack mode. The table was awash with tomato sauce and so were the table's occupants. Nothing on the menu escaped Gran's tackle technique. Spearing a meatball sent the beef orb clear across the table, landing on Dad's lap. She never stopped talking the entire time, skipping from one subject to another like a politician. After the main course I went and made some tea and Mom cleared off the table. The tea made, Mom brought in the plates and one of the combo apple lemon confections. YUMMM. I have to say that the pie was up there with the worst tasting thing I have ever eaten in my life. We all ate up like it was delicious. The Murphy family was nothing if not incredibly polite.

After dinner, I cleaned up so my folks could relax and spend time talking with Gran. By the time I finished cleaning up and joined the oldsters, Gran was nodding off, so Dad got up to get the car keys. Mom put some leftovers in a bag and after some hugs Dad took Gran home. The minute they were out the door my Mom was in the kitchen scraping the leftover pie in the garbage. "That topped all. Truly the worst thing I have ever eaten. I don't even think Mom like it. I was watching her gag down her slice."

Mom and I had another cup of tea and then I went upstairs to get ready for bed.

Chapter 30

Monday was another busy day at work. A lot of the new clients that were at the event on Friday were calling to find out more about what we do. I don't field those kinds of questions. Even though I loved my job, to be honest I still didn't understand why a normal guy would need an escort, bring your wife or girlfriend for crap sake. I get hookers and all that. They offer a tangible service, albeit distasteful, that guys want, but escorts, sorry I don't get it.

There were about six girls that were real money earners for Natasha. These girls were classy, smart and good looking. They were all loyal to Natasha, and appreciated what she did for them. Four of the girls had regular jobs and used the money they earned to supplement their income. A couple of the girls were college seniors and the money they made helped them pay their tuition. Personally, I'd rather work five jobs shoveling shit than be an escort; hanging on some gnarly guy's arm for an evening, grinning like a hyena at the drop of a hat. As if.

At ten o'clock I looked up from my computer and the two beasts were staring at me with leashes in their mouths. So cute. I changed into my runners and took hold of them, called out for Mr. Stoop and Scoop and left the building. When I got to the main park walking with the dogs toward the dog park Gina appeared in front of me. It was like she popped up from nowhere. She scared the shit right out of me. “Yikes, where did you come from? You scared me.” I had pulled the dogs to a halt and they were circling around, and then stopped and stood staring at Gina. “Sorry, I remembered you told me you walked the dogs every day, and because you haven’t returned my calls, I thought I would track you down here at the park.” “Sorry I haven’t called you but I really have nothing to tell you. Besides, I don’t know what you expect of me. I’m a just a summer employee, and a kid I might add. I know nothing,” I said. “I expect you to do you civic duty. I am conducting a police investigation, and you have been asked to cooperate. It wouldn’t be good for you if you don’t help me. The department frowns down on civilians who don’t help police investigations,” Gina said. I wasn’t scared, I was pissed off, she was threatening me and I didn’t like it. Besides I had two huge dogs by my side, what could she do? “Don’t threaten me, I want nothing to do with your so called investigation. I know nothing and I see nothing, got it,” I said. I think I surprised Gina and she was taken aback, “I’m not asking you for anything weird. I wasn’t threatening you I just wanted you to understand the importance of the job. Just answer me this, have you heard from Georgette?” Instead of giving her a long made up explanation I just said, ‘no’ and walked away. “C’mon Coco, c’mon Lola, let’s go to the park.” I turned away shaking with temper and a touch of fear. Mostly I was pissed off, and by the time I got to the dog park I had decided that I was going to call Marcy’s uncle and tell him what had happened. She was threatening me, and if I didn’t have the dogs with me I think she would have tried to hurt me. Mind you, I would have kicked her ass if she laid a hand on me. But who wants to do that. Not this babe.

I let the dogs loose, and after the run and poop, I walked them back to the office.

When I walked into my office Natasha’s door was opened and

Lucius and her were sitting and talking. I popped my head in to say I was back and Natasha said, "Siobhan, can you join us in five minutes?" "Sure, I'll just check for messages and then join you. Do you want some coffee or a soft drink?" I asked. "That would be great. Thanks." I went to the kitchen and put on a pot of coffee and then checked my e-mails and phone messages.

Five minutes later I was ensconced in Natasha's office. "I just got calls from three of my best girls. They quit, just like that, and we don't know why. Did you hear anything?" I sat for a few seconds, "I haven't heard anything not a whisper, nothing. Do they have another job or are they just getting out of the business." I looked at Lucius when I said that but he was completely poker faced. I knew at that exact moment that he poached the girls for his new agency. The prick. "I need your help. Could you talk to the girls and see what they say? I know that's a lot to ask but I want to know what is going on. Maybe their planning on going to work with Georgette when she starts her own place, if she still going to start something that is." It was strange that Natasha was ignoring the fact that Georgette had gone missing, like she was pretending that she never went to her place or anything. Very strange indeed, but I was glad she didn't acknowledge anything about Georgette. I was not happy being asked to do the espionage thing again. "How do I approach them? Just call them and ask if they have time to get together?" I asked. "Probably the straight forward approach is the best way to go. Just ask them straight out, you're good at that. Don't stress yourself about it. But if you can help me, I'd appreciate it," Natasha said. "I'll try my best. Give me a list of the girls and I'll try tracking them down today." Natasha wrote out the names and after a couple of more minutes chatting I left the office.

I got back to my desk and sat staring at my computer screen like it was hypnotizing me, or something weird like that. I really did not want to have coffee with any of these girls. They are so not me, but

I promised Natasha, so I sucked it up and made my first call.

Amy Black was apparently working her way through college. I had never spoken more than a couple of words to her, but she seemed normal, not stuck up or full of herself. She is very good looking in a sophisticated way and well spoken. I called her and got her voice mail. I left a message asking her to call me back on my cell. I didn't go into any detail and pretended as if I knew nothing about her resignation. I called the next two girls on my list and both times my call went to voicemail.

I got back to work and puttered along until noon. I decided to take my lunch to the park. I wanted to call Marcy and tell her about Gina and her threats. I had a lot to do in the next couple of weeks, starting school, choosing courses and generally psyching myself up for the new year of study.

I bought a bottle of water when I got to the park, and sat down with my lunch, took a couple of deep breaths, and then I called Marcy. I told her I was in the park eating lunch, and then told her first about Gina, and what Natasha had told me about the girls leaving. "You have got to be joking. That bitch threatened you, no doubt about it. She actually told you it was your civic duty? Unreal. I'll tell my uncle. You need to watch yourself with that babe. She sounds like a tough customer," Marcy said. "She is and I will be very careful. I called the girls Natasha asked me to call and talk to. Natasha pretended, at least I think she was pretending, that she wasn't aware of Georgette's disappearance. She said she figured that Georgette and her partners had lured them away. She knows that isn't the case. Maybe she did that for Lucius's benefit. Maybe she suspects there's something hairy about the guy, she's pretty sharp," I said. "I'm going to give my uncle a call now and let him know what the scoop is, see what he says or suggests, and I'll let you know. Be real careful what you do and say." After a few minutes more Marcy hung up and I dove into my lunch. I thought about Natasha and wondered to myself if she might already know something fishy is going on. Why would she want the file on Rhode Island so badly if it was a shell company, and she knew the file was empty? Why would she play dumb about Georgette? And why did she want me to check up on Gina in the first place? Does she suspect Gina? Lucius was with her in the office when she asked me to get to know Gina. Lucius must have warned Gina to be on her guard and watch what she says. The two of them probably concocted the whole 'undercover cop' story in the first place. I'm sure they figured I was just some naïve jamoke who would be intimidated completely by the undercover ploy. They were right, of course, I was intimidated and shit scared. Who knew my summer job would be this exciting? What a switch up from a Chew and Choke.

I got back to the office and was working away when I got a call back from Amy Black. I had decided that I was going to take a 'between us gals' approach to finding out why she was leaving and where she was going. I wanted her to think I was asking her out of a combination of idle curiosity and maybe an interest in changing my own job. My deviously brilliant approach worked. We agreed to meet that night. She gave me the name of some coffee place a few blocks away. I toyed with not telling Natasha anything for a couple of reasons, one, I wanted to see how everything played out, and two, I had a feeling that Amy's discretion or lack of it might be a test for her. If Natasha told Lucius that I had a meeting scheduled with Amy it could make things dangerous or scary for Amy.

I decided to get in touch with Conor and check on how the anonymous document gig was going. "Siobhan, I was just going to call you. I have the papers and I am just going over them now. I'll be done by today and will mail them out tomorrow. I'll send your copy to your house. Is that okay? Your parents don't open your mail do they?" I told him my folks wouldn't ever do that. I then told him about the latest developments with Gina and all that. I had to stop talking because Natasha came into the office. “Can I call you tonight?” I said. “Someone just came in right?” he said. “Yep, so I’ll you call later.” I hung up as Natasha approached my desk. “Any word from any of the girls?” I was getting so good at lying, “Not a thing, not yet anyway. I’ll let you know if and when one of them returns my call.” Natasha looked older and kind of sad as she walked back to her office. It made me really angry, and more than determined than ever to help her see what was going on under her nose.

I finished off my work and by five thirty I was cleaning myself up before leaving to meet Amy. I said goodbye to Natasha and left the office. When I got to the coffee shop it looked around and spotted Amy at the back of the place. She was wearing a baseball cap, sunglasses and running gear. I wouldn’t have recognized her if she hadn’t waved me toward her. Incognito, but why?

I sat down and ordered an iced cappuccino and the two of us waited for our orders to arrive before getting down to business. “Thank you for meeting me. You didn’t have to and I appreciate it.” I said. She took off her sunglasses and she was makeup free, not to impressive. I must admit makeup is like magic. She looked butt ordinary. “I was intrigued. Why would you want to know why I left, and why would you care? I don’t know you and you haven’t a clue about me so what gives?” I was kind of shocked by her tone. It was a bit defensive bordering on nasty. How I answered would dictate how long the coffee date would last. “There’s no intrigue or any ulterior motive, I was curious. I just do clerical work for Natasha, and I see all you girls in glamorous clothes, lots of money and all that sort of thing and I wondered why you would give it up. That’s all. I didn’t mean to appear nosey, it’s not my style. I’m sorry if I appeared that way.” Amy sat staring at me for what seemed like forever, I was actually just going to get up and leave when she started to smile. "I'm yanking your chain. It's my righteous indignation act. I couldn't care less why you asked me. It's a job you see, and I got a better offer. Simple as that, I need to make money, I've got bills to pay, and tuition to pony up. I'm studying drama and want to hire a coach a few hours a week and that costs big time. That's why I took a new job, more money and more free time. Don't get me wrong, I like Natasha a lot, she has always been really good to me. She is protective and if a guy tries something out I just let her know and she is on his case and I am off the hook from him completely. But this offer gives me a higher percentage of my hourly rate and they pay medical insurance as well. How cool is that?" "Do you mind telling me where it is you're going?" I asked. She looked at me pretty hard before answering. "It's probably not a good idea for me to tell you, but I will. It's a former client of Natasha's, Lawrence Farber, he's started an agency not far from Natasha's. He said he had several girls signed up including that dimwit broad, Georgette. You have to swear to keep this under your hat. Do not tell anyone or I'll be screwed. He wants to keep it under wraps until the big opening night, next week. Hey maybe I could ask if they have any openings for a clerk. Would you be interested?" Amy asked. "No it's okay, I'm back at school in a few weeks so any job I get has to be very part time. The grand opening is next week huh, that's exciting. You have to let me know how it goes. Do you think you'll get a lot of business there?" I asked. I wanted to drag out the conversation as long as I could by asking as many dumb ass questions as I could dream up. "I think it's going to be great," she said. "I haven't seen Georgette in ages, I guess she's been working with them to help set the place up," I said. "I seriously doubt that. Lawrence said she was a maybe, in terms of new gals but she isn't part of the organizing committee. She's a bit of a lame brain." I felt myself disliking Amy big time. Georgette may be dense, but she had a heart and I couldn't imagine being intentionally mean about anyone. “Well I have to get going. Give me a call once you start at your new place, and tell me how the big night went,” I said. Amy got up with me saying she had to hit the gym before going home. You see that’s the difference between her and I. I had to hit the bakery before I went home.

Chapter 31

I got home, pastry in hand and after handing the delectables off to my Mom I went to change for my Zumba class. I wasn't getting any better at the actual dance part of the class, thanks in part to my two left feet, but I wasn't gasping so much by the end of the class. Marcy and me still parked our butts at the back of the class, eliminating any chance that our lack of dance prowess would get anyone's attention, but at least now we were at the back of the class having a laugh while we were 'working out'. To balance out the calories burned we always went to Anna's for a dinner after. We ate the exact number of calories we burned. It's a 'calories out, calories in' diet philosophy that works for me.

We met up with some of our friends at Anna's and made a night of it. Joking around and gossiping, there's no better way to spend an evening.

After I got home I spent time talking to my Mom and Dad and then went upstairs and changed for bed. It had been quite a day. I wasn't sure what I was going to do next, but one thing was certain I was going to help Natasha. I wondered what the hell had gone on between her and Lucius for him to hatch such an elaborate plot to destroy her. How could you hate someone so much? I didn't think they were lovers anymore but surely they were friends. They had known each other for years, wouldn't that count for something with a guy like Lucius? Maybe there was more to Natasha that I saw, maybe she was a total bitch to him. I seriously doubted it but you never know. I fell asleep dreaming of Natasha, Amy and Marcy's Uncle Frank as well as my Gran and her wacky pies. How the hell do all those characters end up rolled into one weirdo play in my dream. Drives me nuts.

The next day I was sitting at my desk working away like a big old beaver, and Natasha came in with this rather dapper looking older dude. Natasha looked kind of giggly and girly and hung onto him, like he was about to fly away. "Siobhan, I'd like you to meet my friend Stanley Parker. Stanley this is my right hand girl Siobhan." I stood up and shook his hand and he gave me a little bow. Oooh I say, so terribly, Britishly polite. Delighted to meet you Siobhan. That's Irish isn't it, the name Siobhan?" "That's right it's Irish, originally Gaelic, and it means 'gracious', or something like that." After a couple of more awkward moments the two went into Natasha's office. I sat thinking about Natasha and Lucius. Maybe good old Lucius was pissed because Stanley was mowing his lawn, so to speak. Maybe Lucius was hoping he and Natasha would be an item again, and then British Stanley shows up and bing, bang, boom Lucius is kicked to the curb, it's just a theory, but a good one.

I kept my head down until the mail arrived. I was pretty anxious for Natasha to get that anonymous missive so I dove into the mail of course realizing that it wouldn't arrive until tomorrow. I did however find my Mom's thank you note to Natasha, which I put on the top of her pile of mail.

I got back from walking the dogs and called Marcy to see if she could do a search on Lawrence Farber and Stanley Parker. I knew I was being paranoid but I was in up to my teeth and didn't care. "No problem, I'll get right back to you," Marcy said. I swear she is the best at internet searches. It's a science as far as I'm concerned. You have to know what direction you're going so you'll know what path to take. Not something I ever think about, my brain doesn't work like that at all. I'm more of a shoot fish in a barrel, and see what you hit type gal.

True to her word Marcy was back to me an hour later. Apparently Lawrence Farber used to be some cheeseball on Wall Street, but had his ass kicked by the recession. Not a particularly savory type guy. His current job was listed as entrepreneur, whatever that is. What the hell do entrepreneurs do for a living? Are they the free spirit of the business world, is that what it means to be an entrepreneur? It's sort of like calling yourself a philosopher, or a muse. What exactly do these people do? How do you study to be a muse? What courses to you take to be a full time philosopher? Is there a practicum that you do before your finals? Just wondering that's all. I act like such a total ass when I'm nervous, and right now I'm nervous.

She hadn't turned up any poop on Stanley Parker so far, but she said she'd keep on looking. A while later Natasha and Stanley came out of her office, I handed her the mail and she flipped through it and said, "Stan and I are off to lunch. You can reach me at home later if you need me. Oh, is this a note from your mother." She opened my Mom's card and then smiled. "Tell your mom she deserved it. See you tomorrow Siobhan." Natasha giggled and she and Stan the man joked their way out of the office. Lunch and an afternoon assignation between two oldies, it was kind of cute and only a tiny bit gross.

The rest of the afternoon was totally dull and uneventful. I didn't even bother snooping, mostly because I'd done all the snooping I was planning to do, and besides what else was there to look through. I'd pretty much cased the entire room.

I worked away on a couple of new charity events Natasha was putting together for the fall. I was making lists of ideas, attendees, and things we needed to organize. Before long the day was over and I was dragging my ass home.

When I got home I decided to take a quick shower and then spend the night with my folks. After showering and changing into sweats I sat down to dinner. We were sitting around the table talking when the phone rang. Mom answered and handed the phone over to me mouthing Conor's name as she gave me the phone. He asked if he could drop over my copy of the file. I said yes and then hung up. "Conor is dropping something off, he'll be here in a half hour or so." I said and went back to my dessert. My Mom was up out of her seat, racing around to clean up. "Mom, what are you doing I'll clean up later after Conor leaves," I said. "It's okay you go and change and I'll clear away the dishes." Mom said. "Change into what? Why would I change my clothes, I'm comfortable and I look just fine." Mom was looking me up and down, "I think you should spruce yourself up a bit. Put on a little lipstick, a pair of cute jeans and a top, nothing to fussy." I knew she wasn't going to let it go so I relented. My Mom is like a dog with a bone when she wants something, one of her more endearing, and also annoying characteristics. "Okay Mom I'll go change into my First Communion dress, how's that?" Dad was chuckling as he took his plate to the sink and Mom said, "Cheeky monkey, go change."

After changing into my jeans and a t-shirt, and slapping on a swipe of lipstick I went downstairs to wait for Conor. Within in a few minutes there was a knock on the door. I opened it and Conor and his friend were standing there. He handed me the file, "Hi, c'mon in for a coffee," I said. Before he could form a sentence Mom was at the door insisting he come in, "Oh, I'd didn't know you'd brought a pal. Both of you come on in and have some coffee and dessert." They didn't have a chance of refusing my Mom. After a couple of seconds the two were in our living room being shown to seats together.

Mom served some of her lemon meringue pie and Conor's friend raved about it, "How do you get the meringue so high and fluffy, I'd love the recipe." My Mom was surprised by his interest, and she was more than eager to share her baking secrets with him. An hour or so later the two guys got up to leave, "Thank you for the pie Mrs. Murphy, goodnight Mr. Murphy, Mrs. Murphy, Siobhan, we'll be on our way." Conor said. I walked the two to the door and said goodbye.

The minute I got back to the living room my Dad said, "Was that guy a bit poofy or am I all wet?" I started to laugh, my Mom was totally mortified, "Of course he wasn't poofy, he just likes to bake that's all." My parents aren't homophobic at all. I don't think they even know what homophobic means. They are what I call 'the curious straight'. My Dad thinks it's odd but couldn't care less what your persuasion is, and Mom believes in the 'whatever makes you happy' philosophy. After listening to the two of them banter back and forth I kissed them both goodnight and went to my room. Within seconds Conor called me, "I hope that we were okay. I didn't expect to come in for dessert and coffee." "Don't worry, my parents never thought anything. Although asking for my Mom's recipe for meringue was a bit edgy but they are so not suspicious. I've already told you I think you should be up front with your folks, but don't worry they'll never hear anything about your sexual orientation from my parents," I said. "Thanks Siobhan. I know you're right, and I'll do it but I have to work up to it." "Hey you know them best and it's certainly your call. Thanks for the file. Did you mail the copy to Natasha?" I asked. "Yep, it went out first thing this morning. She should have it tomorrow or the next day. Let me know when it arrives. Talk to you soon."

Chapter 32

When I got to the office I felt really nervous for some reason. I guess the prospect of that file arriving in the mail made me antsy. I made coffee and sat at my desk, I was way to fidgety to do anything. Natasha arrived ten minutes later and had a big grin on her face when she walked in. I guess Stanley is now her main man. I was glad because she was looking so unhappy a few days ago. I'm so worried how she'll react when she gets the file. "Good morning Siobhan, how are you on this beautiful summer day?" Before I got a chance to answer she sailed into her office. I went and got her a coffee and when I returned the mail had arrived. The envelope from Conor was right on top. I sorted the mail and brought it in to Natasha. My heart was pounding out of my chest. "Get your coffee and come and join me." Shit I was going to be sitting in front of her when she opened the envelope. I went and got my coffee and when I walked back into her office she was opening the envelope. "What's this?" She said as I sat down in front of her. Without looking at me she read the file, she then looked up at me and said, "Call my lawyer Siobhan, tell him to get here immediately. Do not let anyone else into the office. Let Jenkins walk the dogs by himself." I left the room and called her lawyer right away. "She wants you here right away. When can you get here?" I asked. He told me he would be at the office in a half hour. I went back and told Natasha he was on his way. "Thanks Siobhan, come in and sit with me." "Do you want more coffee?" I asked. "Sure bring in the service and a cup for George Kelly." When I returned with the service Lucius was walking through the door and toward Natasha's office. "Natasha doesn't want to be disturbed. I'll tell her you're here." He glared at me and kept on walking towards her office, "Get lost little girl. I'll do as I please." I followed him into the office. Natasha stood up and said, "Oh sorry Lucius, I told Siobhan to keep everyone out. I'll call you later I have a few personal things I need to do." As she was speaking to him I remembered George Kelly was on his way. I looked at Natasha and then raced out to the lobby just as he was coming in. "Mr. Kelly come into the boardroom Natasha will be with you in a minute." I raced back to her office as Lucius was leaving. "Sorry I was nasty to you. Nothing personal right?" Lucius said. I smiled and showed him to the door and watched him go out the front door. I ran back to the boardroom and got the lawyer and brought him into Natasha's office. "Thank you for coming on such short notice George. Come sit down, help yourself to coffee." I was on my way out the door and Natasha said, "Stay Siobhan, I want you here with me. I need you." I was paralyzed, I wanted out of that room so bad, but I gulped and took a seat.

Natasha said nothing and pushed the file to George Kelly, "What's this?" "I'm not sure but I thought you might know." Natasha said. George opened the file and studied it, and then looked up, "What's this all about. Rhode Island is a dead, shell company. Why did you buy a building under the name and company?" "I didn't George, I thought you might know what is going on, but it appears you're also in the dark." Natasha said. "Where did you get this document from?" George asked. "It arrived today, anonymously. No note attached, nothing just the file. Tell me what you think this is about. Tell me what you think this means." George thought about it for a few seconds and said, "Well if you didn't buy the building, someone did, using your company and your money, at least I think it's your money. If you don't know anything about this then we need to act fast." "The only person who has access to anything is Lucius. No one else knows anything about my business." I hadn't said a word yet, "If you don't mind, I think you should go to this address right now. You need to see what's going on." Natasha and George looked at me, "You're right. Let's go now," Natasha said. "We'll take a cab, that way we won't attract any attention," George said. Minutes later the three of us were on our way.

By now the lump in my throat was the size of a grapefruit and the butterflies in my stomach were fluttering around like crazy. I felt totally nervous and nauseated at the same time. I can't imagine how Natasha must have felt. The trip to the building was totally silent.

We got there and the cab barely slowed down to a stop and Natasha was out of the door. "Natasha, wait for us." She slowed down and the three of us walked up to the door. George knocked and then tried the door. It was unlocked and we walked in just as Lucius was walking into the lobby. "What the hell? What are you doing here?" Natasha walked up to Lucius and slapped him across the face so hard he stepped back with the impact. Just as he was giving his head a shake Lawrence Farber came into the lobby with Gina behind him. The two of them stopped in their tracks. "You must think I'm completely stupid. I see what you people are doing. My mistake was that I trusted you Lucius. You'll all pay for this. Since this is my building, I'm shutting it down. Get out of here now or I'll call the police. I plan on doing that later as soon as I figure out what you've done. Get out!" The three of us stood there staring at the three of them, it was almost like a standoff. After a few seconds they turned and walked out of the building.

Natasha stood in the centre of the lobby and she looked so lost and upset. I went up to her and put my arms around her. "I'm so sorry you have been betrayed. What can I do?" Natasha had tears in her eyes when she looked at me but after a few seconds the tears were replaced by what appeared to be fury. "Siobhan, find a hardware store and purchase a chain and padlock. George and I will bolt the door until you return. C'mon George let's see if we can find some of their paperwork." I left the building looking around to make sure none of the guilty party were waiting in the bushes, ready to pounce on me. I'm so dramatic. After checking the area I legged it to a hardware store a couple of blocks away.

When I got back to the building I had to bang on the door really hard before George opened it up. "Come on into the office." I followed him and we went to the office on the second floor. Natasha was sitting at a desk with a pile of files in front of her. "Let's take these back to the office. Siobhan, can you go through the computer and copy anything that looks pertinent to disk." I got right to it and within an hour I had gone through and copied everything that looked business related. I also spotted a list of clients on a spreadsheet. It looked like amounts beside their names so I copied it and forwarded it to my e-mail address.

The three of us bundled up all of the files into bags and went down to the lobby. After a quick look around we left the building and George applied the padlock I had bought. We stood together like a tight little group, each looking in the direction in front of them. George hailed a cab and when it arrived we were driven back to the office. Natasha told Jenkins to ask everyone to leave the building including himself and then lock the door after himself.

Natasha went to the boardroom with George. I went to my office to check for messages and after I took a quick look through the list I had forwarded to my e-mail address, I printed it off. It was indeed, a list of clients and amounts, and my new philosophy just kicked into high gear – if it looks like a duck, walks like a duck, quacks like a duck, it's a duck.

I walked into the boardroom and handed the spreadsheet to Natasha, "What's this?" I explained that I had forwarded it to my e-mail because I wasn't sure what it was until I opened it up. Natasha handed the sheet to George, "Looks like your friend Lucius was playing a dangerous game of blackmail," George said. It was at this point that I thought I would leave the two of them to do what they had to do. "I can leave you two if you want me to. I know all this is pretty confidential and I'm just an assistant." I had said it a flip and hopefully uncloying way – is 'uncloying even a word? The fact was, I wanted to get the hell out of the whole thing, I'm just a kid and it was just a summer job after all.

Natasha and George looked up from the papers, "I would like you to stay. If you feel awkward or anything like that then by all means you can go, but you're part of this team and I really appreciate your help and opinion." Natasha said. How could I refuse, I wanted to see what would happen, and I wanted to see Lucius and his gang get their butts kicked. "Of course I'll help in anyway I can. What do you want me to do?" Natasha said, "First let's get the phone numbers of these guys on the spread sheet as well as the charity they have donated to. I want to know what they gave and how often they used our service. I also want to know which girls they had as escorts." "I suspect the girls they had are the same ones that are leaving your company," George said. "Do we have a list of the girls that Lucius has hired?" Natasha asked. George and I went through the files and found a list of phone numbers and names. "This looks like some sort of list. I see Amy is on the list as well as Louise and Linda the other two that resigned," I said.

Everything seemed like such a mess, and I had no idea what the next move was and then I remembered, "Natasha, what about your condo? Does Lucius have a key to your condo?" I asked. If he did he could be there right now tearing the place apart. Having a hairy fit or something. "Yes, yes he does. He's probably there right now. What'll I do?" George and I spoke almost in unison, "Call the police." "I also think you need to call the doorman or the office or whatever you have there and warn them." George said. Natasha went away to call her building and the police and I said, "George, shouldn't we be calling the police? What he did was illegal and the longer we wait to tell the police the more they will think that Natasha had something to do with it. I think we should call right away." George was looking at the paperwork and then turned to me, "You're right but we need to see how Natasha is implicated before we do anything." Just then Natasha returned. "The doorman told me that Lucius has just gone up to the condo. He said a couple of other people were with him. I told him to let the police into my condo as soon as they arrive." "We were just talking, we think you need to get the police involved right away. You will appear involved somehow if you don't tell them what has gone on. You have to tell them everything otherwise you'll be on the hook. Lucius was smart. Everything is in your name. The men he was blackmailing probably believe that it's you who is behind it all. They wouldn't think anyone else was involved. Calling the police will send a message saying, 'I just found out and am acting immediately." Failure to act right away could make them think you are covering something up." George said. Natasha nodded her head, "I agree, Siobhan call the police."

I left the boardroom and went to my office to make the call. The thing was I didn't want Natasha to know I had been doing an investigation behind her back. I wanted to contact Marcy's uncle and tell him what had transpired and ask him to keep quiet about my involvement.

After waiting a few minutes I got Uncle Frank on the phone and told him the whole story, "No worries, your story is safe with me. Thanks for the heads up though it looks like you were right. We'll be there in ten minutes. I heard that police have been dispatched to your boss's condo. Is that right?" I told him it was and thanked him for keeping everything to himself. I went back to the boardroom to tell Natasha and George that the police were on their way. "Thanks Siobhan. We should probably bring all the books and paper work in here. What do you think George?" "Let's speak with the police first and then they can tell us what they require." "I'm going to get some coffee and sandwiches for us, is that okay?" I asked. "Good idea, get a receipt, and thanks Siobhan, you've been a big help."

I went to my office and got my purse and my phone. I wanted to call Marcy and tell her what was going on. I was like a bit of a jerk for not telling Natasha my suspicions in the first place. At least she found out so that was a good thing. As I opened the door to leave Uncle Frank and a couple of other detectives were walking up the stairs. I went back inside with them and showed them to the boardroom. "The police are here Natasha. I'll be back shortly. Did you guys want anything to eat?" I asked. They said they didn't and I left. I decided to take the dogs with me just in case they needed to use the facilities.

Besides they were pretty formidable protection. You never know maybe Gina or one of her people, whoever 'her people' are, may be waiting to pounce on me.

I got to the deli and ordered my sandwiches and some cookies for the cops, and said I would be back to pick them up in ten minutes. I walked the dogs over to the dog park and just as I was about to let them off leash Gina turned up. "Well, well, well, if it isn't our little teenage detective. I thought I would find you here." She came close to me and she had her hand in her pocket. Of course I immediately assumed it was a gun and started to scream my lungs off. The dogs were on it in a second and I pointed to Gina and they pounced on her and knocked her down. In the meantime a beat cop came running over, "What's going on kid?" I told him that Gina had threatened me and the dogs jumped her. "Check her pocket for a gun. She gestured like she had one in her pocket that's why I screamed," I said. The dogs still had her pinned to the ground and so I pulled them off her and the cop pulled her to her feet and then told her to empty her pockets on the ground. Sure enough she took out a gun from her pocket. I briefly explained what had transpired and told him that police were back at my office. He said he would come to the office after he took Gina down to the station and booked her. I gave him my office address and left to go back to the deli. I was amazed at my cool, calm and rapier quick reflexes, I'm just a kid, who knew I could be so controlled. I should be shaking like a leaf right now but I'm picking up sandwiches for my boss. Very cool.

I got back to the brownstone and went straight through to the boardroom. Everyone was still there and so I told them what had happened. Natasha was appalled, "Oh my god, you could have been killed. If anything happened to you I would never, ever forgive myself." "Natasha, it's okay I had the dogs with me, and when I realized what her game was I screamed blue murder, and set the dogs on her. Believe me she didn't have a chance. Besides, why would she approach me in a crowded park? She must be desperate or just plain stupid. By the way the policeman who came to the park is on his way here after he books her," I said. "You seem to have everything under control miss," one of the cops said. I told him I was merely doing my civic duty. Could you gag, I swear I am such an A-hole at times.

After taking statements and signing for all the paperwork that was taken from the other building the cop who rescued me had arrived. He told us all that there had been a couple of men go to the condo and removed Lawrence Farber and Lucius. "Our guys got there as the two were loading up some bags with whatever was around that looked like it had some value. The older guy said it was his stuff and he was just packing it away. Of course we knew better and had them removed and brought down to the station."

Everyone talked for another half hour or so and then one of the detectives said, "We're going to have to call these people and see if they are willing to press charges or let us investigate. The problem is they probably believe it's you who is behind the blackmail and that's a big problem for you. Your friend Lucius was very smart. He did the whole thing, the building purchase, money transfers, blackmailing and even stealing some of your employees, right under your nose and in your name. If you hadn't received that anonymous file you would never have known. He would have drained your company dry and then took off with all of your money." Natasha looked shocked and suddenly every second her age. Her eyes filled up with tears and I went over to sit with her. I put my arm around her and said, "C'mon let's go and clean up a bit and then we're going to make those SOB's pay for what they did." I took her to her office and she went to her bathroom and splashed water on her face, reapplied some makeup, touched up her hair and came back looking much better. "Thanks Siobhan. I was feeling a little sorry for myself but I'm over it. Now I'm just plain angry."

We got back to the boardroom just as the police were packing up the paperwork and files we had brought from the other building. "We'll be in touch in a day or so. The first thing we're going to do is contact the people on the list. I have doubts whether any of them will admit to being blackmailed but we'll wait and see."

After the police left George and Natasha sat discussing what they were going to do next. "I think you have to decide what you want to do with that building you appear to own. You also need to decide how you will proceed with the men who have been paying blackmail money. Do you contact them personally and apologize or try and make amends or do you just leave it to the police." Natasha sat and thought about it and then I said, "Those guys were doing stuff they weren't supposed to do. Granted the girls were part of it but still why should you apologize. You can give them their money back once everything is sorted, but you don't owe those creepy guys an apology. That's my two cents worth." Both Natasha and George were staring at me and then Natasha started to laugh, "You're right Siobhan. They were doing something they weren't supposed to do. I have no need to apologize. I'll certainly reimburse them when I get the money back from the sale of the building, but that's where the whole thing ends. I don't want them as clients anyway."

I was bushed and I stood up and said, "I'm going to go home now. I'm feeling really tired and I think I'd better spend time telling my parents what's happened. Is that okay with you Natasha?" "It is but I would like to come with you and explain. I feel like I need to apologize to your folks and assure them everything is going to be fine. Is that okay? We'll get a cab in a couple of minutes." I was kind of surprised that Natasha wanted to come home with me, but maybe it was a good idea. I told her I was going to phone my folks so they wouldn't be surprised.

Chapter 33

My Mom was waiting for us when we got to the house. Natasha walked in and I followed, "So nice to meet you Mrs. Murphy. Thank you for letting me visit." Natasha said. "Please call me Mary and it's lovely to meet you. Come on into the kitchen I have coffee and a cake all ready."

Over the next hour Natasha explained what went on and my role in it. She also told my Mom how glad she was that I was on her side. "Your daughter is a one of a kind kid, and it was a great day for me when she came to work in the office." I was blushing like a bandit. My Mom joined in the Siobhan mutual admiration society. "My girl is a one of a kind kid. She's our pride and joy." Natasha had a smile on her face and a bit of a tear in her eyes. Mom, got up and went over and gave her a big hug. "Everything is going to be just fine. I'm sure of it. Good people always win, and your good people. Now then can you stay for dinner?" Natasha stood up, "You know Mary I would love to but I have some things to get settled but perhaps another time if you'll invite me again."

Mom and me walked Natasha to the door when her cab came and she said, "Will I see you tomorrow Siobhan?" "Of course, I'll be in bright and early." My Mom said, "I'm making the two of you a nice big lunch. Meatloaf sandwiches are good for the soul and good for you." After Natasha got in her cab, Mom and me walked into the kitchen,"I'm proud of you honey. You're a good kid and you're completely fearless. Your Dad and me know how to raise a good one. That's for sure"

I helped clean up the kitchen and then said, "I'm going to call Marcy. I'll set the table later Mom. Is that okay?" "Go ahead and don't worry about setting the table. I'll look after it." I gave Mom a kiss and raced to my room to call Marcy. I knew she would be sitting on the edge of her seat waiting for my call. When I called earlier in the day I gave her almost no information. "I'm on my way over. I want to hear the whole ugly story from the beginning."

I called Conor next and told him part of what went down. "Holy, that is unreal. You guys actually walked into the building and took over. It's a like a coup in a small country. So cool." Not exactly how I would characterize the action, but clearly Conor doesn't get out a whole hell of a lot. I hung up after promising to fill him in on all the gory details later. I could hear Marcy downstairs saying 'hi' to Mom, and then I went to meet Marcy at my door. Once inside I closed the door. "OMG, I cannot believe what you had to go through. Was it exciting? Were you scared? Spill." "I was shit scared, are you kidding? It was exciting, but I'm so glad it's over believe me." I told Marcy about Gina and after laughing at the vision of Gina on the ground and the dogs on top of her. "That 'beeatch' actually threatened you? She really had a gun and was going to use it? What the hell for? You didn't do anything to provoke her at all. Why would she threaten you like that?" "I haven't a clue. I never did anything to her. I stopped meeting her and maybe that was it. I think Gina has a really bad temper and doesn't like to lose, she threatened me because she was so pissed off. I think she thought I was going to cringe and shake because I'm a kid. She's like a total sociopath or something. I suppose she thought I'd be a pushover. I also think she is a total bully and a mean bitch. I can tell you one thing for sure the dogs came in real handy," I said. "Well she doesn't know Siobhan, that's for sure. What do you think Natasha will do now? Will she shut down her business? What about the other building that she apparently owns? Do you think she'll keep it or sell it?" Talk about being cross-examined. Marcy doesn't cut corners when she asks questions. You have to laugh. "I don't have a clue what Natasha is going to do. I have a feeling she will sell the other building and give the money to the guys Lucius was blackmailing. Other than that, I have no idea what's next."

Marcy stayed for dinner and then the two of us met some friends and just hung out. Normal is good. After I got home, did the 'hey' with my folks' I went to my room and crashed. I was totally wacked. I slept like a dead person.

I woke up early and after I got ready I went to the kitchen and had a Murphy buffet for breakfast. "You need to be very careful Siobhan. You never know who is lurking around the corner. Do you want Dad to drive you to work?" "Mom, the police are all over it. Everyone who was involved is in jail or being charged. Don't worry about me, I'll be fine." I said. "I do worry, and I will always worry. Be careful that's all I'm saying." My Mom and Dad kept on about dangerous people and all that crap so much that by the time I left the house, and arrived at work my neck was sore from looking over my shoulders.

Natasha was in her office when I arrived. "Hi Natasha, can I get you some coffee and something to eat?" I asked. "Good morning Siobhan, I'd love a coffee, get one for yourself and come join me. We have a lot to talk about." I made up a tray of coffee and cookies and brought it into Natasha's office. I poured the coffee and the two of us drank in silence. "What are you going to do about the business? Are you going to keep it opened?" I asked. The summer was nearly over so losing my peach of a job didn't concern me as much as what would happen to Natasha. I'm such a friggin' saint I can't stand myself. "The first thing I need to do is extricate myself from all this trouble with the blackmail and fraud. The problem, of course, is that everything is in my name. I have been stupid, and I trusted people to look after my interests. I assumed loyalty where none existed. I think I will operate a company but I'm not sure the escort business is the type of company I want to own or run any longer." "You weren't stupid. What reason would you have for not trusting Lucius? You've known him for a long time, and he was a hell of an actor. He gave me the impression he was devoted to you," I said. "Thanks Siobhan. I appreciate what you said. I still should have watched over the books and the banking more carefully. Anyway, what's done is done," Natasha said. "What sort of business do you think you will start?" As long as she didn't say she wanted to open a brothel, I wanted to work for her. "I was thinking about event planning. We do so much of it anyway, and I know what I'm doing. I have contacts and deals with every venue in the city, I know all the florists, lighting specialists and entertainers and their agents, and I know how to throw a great party. What do you think?" I was smiling like crazy, "I think it's an awesome plan. You would be phenomenal in that business." "First things first, I need to extricate myself from all this garbage that has happened, sell that building and then set about reorganizing my life and business. I hope you can continue to work for me Siobhan. I know you are returning to school in a couple of weeks but you can work part-time during the school year," Natasha said. "I was hoping you'd ask. I would love to keep working for you."

After we sorted out the day's schedule Natasha called her lawyer George and I set about calling all the girls to tell them they had to look for another job. For the most part they couldn't care less. A couple asked about what Natasha was planning on doing next, and almost all of them wanted to know what Natasha was